"Chelsea, what is it?
What are you so afraid of?"

Chelsea couldn't answer Ricardo. He would laugh. No, her fears didn't make much sense, even to herself. Nevertheless, they were real.

Ricardo's eyes moved slowly up to the taut peaks of her breasts. "You want me, Chelsea, right now. Have you any idea what it's going to be like for us when we do make love?"

"We're not going to be lovers—ever." Her voice was a whisper.

"Oh, but we are." Ricardo spoke gravely. "It's been there all along, this attraction. It won't be denied."

He was right! Chelsea recognized the truth when she heard it. "Please get out," she murmured.

He smiled. "Relax, Chelsea. You're one woman I'm not interested in seducing. You have to meet me halfway. I'll wait."

CLAUDIA JAMESON lives in Berkshire, England, with her husband and family. She is an extremely popular author in both the Harlequin Presents and Harlequin Romance series. And no wonder! Her lively dialogue and ingenious plots—with the occasional dash of suspense—make her a favorite with romance readers everywhere.

Books by Claudia Jameson

Don't miss any of our special offers. Write to us at the following address for information on our newest releases.

Harlequin Reader Service
901 Fuhrmann Blvd., P.O. Box 1397, Buffalo, NY 14240
Canadian address: P.O. Box 603,
Fort Erie, Ont. L2A 5X3

CLAUDIA JAMESON

to speak of love

Harlequin Books

TORONTO • NEW YORK • LONDON
AMSTERDAM • PARIS • SYDNEY • HAMBURG
STOCKHOLM • ATHENS • TOKYO • MILAN

Harlequin Presents first edition April 1987
ISBN 0-373-10969-5

Original hardcover edition published in 1986
by Mills & Boon Limited

CHAPTER ONE

'MADRID? You're going to *Madrid*? But—but that's the other side of the world!' And that was precisely where Chelsea Prescott had just come from. Well, almost. She had come from Europe, anyway. Her flight from London, England, had arrived at J. F. Kennedy airport in New York less than an hour ago ... and now she was being informed by her father that he was taking off for Spain the day after tomorrow. 'Oh, *Daddy*!'

She looked at her father in despair, but for once Hal Prescott was not prepared even to listen to her. He pressed the button which would close the glass partition between them and the driver of the limousine, his voice calm and quiet—and unmoved. 'It's your own fault. If you'd called me first, I could have told you what my plans are. Really, Chelsea, you should know better. You know the sort of life I lead. What a crazy thing to do—just hopping on a plane to New York without even talking to me first! You do realise you've got here nine days early?' He frowned, searching her face, as though all this might be a stupid mistake on her part.

Obviously it was. But no, she hadn't got her dates mixed up. She had flown to New York because, after the fight she'd had with her mother, there was nowhere else for her to go—except back to school, which was the last thing she wanted.

She turned her attention to the traffic belting along the freeway in the same direction as her father's limousine, her eyes flicking unseeingly from cars to trucks and then further ahead to the enormously high buildings which made up the dramatic skyline of Manhattan. It was made even more dramatic now by the pink-blue hues of the setting sun. She liked New

York well enough but she didn't really feel that she belonged here. She didn't *belong* anywhere. And her father was right, of course: she shouldn't have come without warning him, *asking* him. If she wanted to see her parents, either of them, she had to make appointments with them; that had always been the case, ever since she had been a little girl.

It used to hurt terribly, this feeling of not belonging ... to either her mother or her father, to any place in particular ... but she was hardened to it now. She had never understood her parents and their crazy marriage that was not a marriage. She was an only child, her mother was English, her father American and they had separated, but not divorced, years ago. Ten years ago, to be precise, when Chelsea was seven years old. From then on they had lived in their respective countries and Chelsea had been at boarding schools in England, seeing her parents only during the holidays. Was it any wonder she didn't understand them? Was it any wonder they were strangers to her? They always had been. Nothing had changed; if she wanted to see her mother, it necessitated a train journey of several hours from her school to her mother's home, which was a health farm in Torquay, in the South of England. If she wanted to see her father, it involved a flight across the Atlantic to New York. So no, nothing had changed except that these days she travelled alone, without some 'Universal Aunt' to accompany her. Thank God she was seventeen now, almost eighteen. She was grown up ... And it was this that had caused the row between her and her mother.

It was Easter. Within a few short months her exams would be behind her and she would be leaving school. At last! Come summer, when the results of her A-levels would be to hand, she would have something with which to make a start in the world She already had six O-levels and was confident of passing at least three A-levels. And then ... well, then she would decide what to do with her life. Quite what she wanted to do, she wasn't sure. The only talent she had was her ability with languages. That was a real talent—or so people told her. For the moment, she knew only that she was *not* going to be packed off to yet another educational establishment—of *any* description.

'Chelsea? I'm talking to you! I said——'

'I heard you.' She turned to face her father, surprised by the harshness of his tone. Normally he treated her as though she were a pet, and he usually called her 'Princess'.

There had been a time when that had made her feel special to him—but not any more. Normally he was extremely patient with her, always ready to listen, unlike her mother. Yet he'd always won in the end, whenever she'd argued with him in the past. But not any more! He wouldn't win this time.

Materially, financially, he spoiled her, and there had been a time when she had mistaken that for love. But she didn't now. She felt *angry*, with him, with her mother, with the entire world. Nobody gave a damn, including her parents. Especially her parents. 'Of course I realise I'm nine days early!' For the first time in her life she actually yelled at her father and there was a great satisfaction in seeing the look of astonishment on his face.

'Good heavens, child, what's happened?' So he had paused, at last, to ask himself this question!

'My mother and I had a fight.'

Hal Prescott relaxed against the plush leather upholstery. 'So, what else is new?' When there was no answer, he looked again at his daughter, he looked hard and long this time. Her emotions were not difficult to fathom. He could see anger, resentment and something approaching bitterness. What he couldn't understand was why it all seemed to be directed at *him*. It disturbed him. He reached for her hand. 'Hey, come on, Princess. What's wrong?'

It gushed out of her as she snatched her hand away. 'What's wrong? What's *wrong*? The reception you've given me this evening, that's what's wrong! The fact that you don't give a damn about me and never have. That what's wrong!'

'Chelsea! Just because I have to go away——'

'I'm not talking about that! I know I'm early for my Easter holday *appointment* with you, but why didn't your stupid secretary say something when I phoned? Didn't she tell you I called from the airport in London and . . .' She faltered. From Heathrow airport she had spoken to her father's secretary because he had been out at a business luncheon. But he had obviously been given the message that his daughter was on her way to see him. He'd been at the airport to meet her, he hadn't merely sent his driver with the car.

Big deal! 'So why didn't your secretary tell me you were scheduled to go to Madrid the day after tomorrow? I wouldn't have come here if I'd realised.'

But there had been nowhere else to go. She couldn't have stayed on with her mother, not after their row. She wished, now, that she'd accepted Carmen Romero's offer of holidaying with her and her parents in Scotland. Carmen was her best friend in school, and the offer had been tempting. But Chelsea had declined because it was vitally important she talk to her parents about her future. Her *future*, for heaven's sake. *Her* future. She had wanted to tell them it was *not* going to be the way they'd planned it for her, that she was *not* going to spend the next year in some dumb finishing school and four years after *that* in some boring university.

And what had she achieved so far? Nothing. All she'd had so far was abuse from her mother and the news that her father was going away on business. Right, then she would damn well wait here till he got back!

'Because you didn't give her the chance to tell you, that's why. You hung up too quickly.' Her father was being patient again, more like his usual self. Actually, he was bemused by the look on Chelsea's face. He'd never seen her this angry before. 'Look, Princess, it's not that important. You're here now and I'm very glad to see you. That's all that matters isn't it?'

Again, Hal reached for her hand. While there was no answer from her, at least she didn't snatch her hand away this time. Suddenly she seemed younger than ever to him and he tightened his grip reassuringly. There was still no response. 'Come on, it's no big deal. You'll come to Madrid with me,' he added positively.

'I will not! I——' She stopped dead, suspicious. Her immediate response had been made without thought. Her father hadn't asked her about going with him to Madrid, he'd told her. You'll come with me. How typical. But—heavens, this was a turn up for the book! Her apple-green eyes narrowed again in suspicion. 'I thought . . . I thought you were going to Spain on *business*?'

'I am.'

She was incredulous. 'And you want me to go with you?'

'Yes.' He was smiling now.

'But——' She couldn't say anything else. He meant it! The rush of gladness she felt brought a broad grin to her face and for the moment, she couldn't think of anything else to say. This was unheard of, unprecedented! Nothing, but nothing, ever got in the way of business—with either of her parents. Yet here was her father, wanting to take her to Madrid when she would surely represent a potential distraction to him.

As the limousine made its way through Manhattan, Chelsea's mood changed to one of buoyancy. Her anger vanished, her resentment of her father lessened enormously and she became suddenly interested in the days that would follow. Madrid! She'd never been anywhere in Spain, and her first glimpse would be of the capital!

Her questions came in a bombardment. 'What time

will we fly? Where are we staying? At some splendid
hotel? And how long for? Will it be worth my while
coming back here afterwards or——'

'Hey, hey, hey!' Her father held up a defensive hand.
'Give a guy a chance!'

Chelsea clamped her mouth together, the tips of two
white teeth digging into her lower lip as she grinned
again, eyes bright with happiness now. 'Sorry!'

Hal couldn't help laughing. Without bias he could
say she was a pretty child, so much like her mother with
those bright green eyes and hair the colour of chestnuts.
All that and a delightful scattering of freckles, too.
'We'll be there for about four or five days. So yes, it will
be worth your while coming back to New York with me
afterwards. We'll have our vacation together, as
planned. I'll have to spend a couple of days back in the
bank first, but then we'll go to the beach house on the
day we're supposed to.' He drew a deep breath, teasing
her now, as though he were trying to answer her
questions as quickly as she'd asked them. 'No, we're
not staying in a "splendid" hotel, not even in an
ordinary one, but we are staying in a rather splendid
house. Señor Colchero's house. Do you remember him?
Ramón Colchero?'

Chelsea remembered him. She had a clear mental
picture of him, a middle-aged man who had once come
to dinner at her father's apartment when she had been
there. She remembered not only because the Spaniard's
presence had necessitated her father having to go into
work the next day, when he was supposed to be on
holiday, but also because Señor Colchero had been so
sweet to her.

How old had she been at the time? Eleven? Twelve?
And he had been a jovial man, tall, stout, with steel-
grey hair and a jet-black moustache—a striking
combination. A man who had laughed a lot, at least
with her, that was what she remembered now. He
certainly wasn't everyone's image of a banker, not even

a merchant banker. But a merchant banker was what he was . . . or rather, had been.

She looked at her father solemnly as the car finally turned on to Fifth Avenue. They were almost home but she wasn't thinking about that. She was thinking about the letter she'd got from her father only three months earlier. The arrival of his letters was easy to remember because they were so rare. In this one, he had mentioned the death of Ramón Colchero, a man he had known many years, a good friend as well as business associate. That was how Hal had worded the letter. 'Yes, I remember him clearly, Daddy. I—you never said how he died.'

'From a heart attack. It was just like that.' Her father clicked his fingers. 'Actually it was his third attack. He should have taken things much easier than he did. He was only fifty-five, you know.'

Chelsea gave him a swift look. Her father was forty-five. What was he thinking? That maybe he should take things easier, too? Not a chance! 'So who's taken over his place in the bank? I mean, how come we're staying at his house when——'

'One of his brothers has taken over as Chairman.'

'And the brother lives in the house where we're staying?'

'No, he has his own family. Ramón's children live in the house, and his old mother. She's a lovely lady. Ramón has . . . had . . . two sons and a daughter. The younger son is at university, the elder works for the bank, of course.'

'Why do you say "of course"?'

There was a slight smile. 'It's almost a tradition with them, the Colcheros, I mean. The family own the bank outright. They're descendants of nobility, you know, they go back hundreds of years.'

Chelsea's father was a director of a large American banking organisation. Señor Colchero had been the chairman of a merchant bank. The two organisations

sometimes did business together. That was all she
knew, or cared to know. The world of banking seemed
like a dead bore to her. So did bankers, on the whole.
Except for the jovial Spaniard. Fancy his family owning
the bank outright! 'Wow! The Colcheros must be
absolutely *loaded*!'

She leant forward as the car slowed down, glancing
up at the smart building in which her father had a large,
modern apartment overlooking Central Park. Hal
Prescott had done extremely well for himself in his
profession, having started out with next to nothing in
life. Chelsea knew that he had begun his career, many
years ago, as a mere teller with the bank he was now a
director of. There was no inherited money in the
Prescott family.

Hal nodded as the doorman of the building came
forward to open the doors for them. 'What will be of
interest to you is that Ramón's daughter is just your
age. I think you'll get on well with her. I spoke to her
about you when I went over for Ramón's funeral. I
hadn't seen her for a long time, she's turned out to be a
very pretty girl. Her name's Mercedes, by the way,
and . . .'

And then he spoiled everything completely. He
slipped an arm around Chelsea's shoulders as they
walked into the building, looking down at her as
though she would be delighted by what he had to tell
her next. '. . . and you'll be surprised to learn that you
and she are going to be classmates. Yes, that's right!
She's going to the same finishing school as you in the
fall. Won't that be nice?'

Everything came back, the anger, the resentment, the
frustration. Why, he was almost patting her on the head
now, as though she were three years old, not seventeen!
Won't that be nice.

Like hell!

But she said nothing, the time wasn't right. Besides,
she was tired, tired from thinking so much, tired from

the fight with her mother, tired from the journey. As far as she was concerned, it was midnight now, not seven in the evening. She was also very hungry.

She stiffened as her father's arm continued to rest on her shoulders when they stepped into the lift—or rather the elevator, as she would call it now she was back in the United States. 'Do you mind, Daddy?' She moved away from him, avoiding his eyes.

Now what was the matter with her? 'Chelsea? You'll enjoy yourself, darling, I promise. I'm sure you'll find Mercedes very good company. That's why I'm taking you to Madrid with me—because you'll have someone to talk to. I know your Spanish is good enough.'

She looked down at the carpeted floor. So that was it. What he meant was that she'd be out of his hair. She should have known there was a catch, that he didn't *really* want her to go with him.

Later, later she would tell him a thing or two. It could wait until after dinner. She forced herself to smile then; there was no point in behaving childishly when shortly she had to convince him of her maturity. 'Sorry, Pop. I'm—just tired, that's all.'

'And hungry, I'll bet?' He was smiling again, oblivious to the fact that there was so much going on in her head—so *much*.

Hal glanced at his watch as the doors opened and the elevator man picked up Chelsea's suitcase. The arm came around her shoulders again. 'Mrs Freer will have dinner ready for you. I'll see you settled in but I'm afraid I can't eat with you. I have to go out to dinner. It's business, you know . . .'

Chelsea didn't get a chance to talk to her father the following day, either. Her body-clock had been thrown out of sync and she woke at four the next morning. Of course, it was nine o'clock as far as she was concerned. Nine o'clock English time. With a groan, she thumped her pillow and went back to sleep. The next thing she knew, it was almost seven.

Her father was dressed and eating breakfast when she joined him. 'Sleep well?' He glanced at her over a copy of *The Wall Street Journal* and was back to reading it before she even answered.

She helped herself to a cup of coffee and refused Mrs Freer's offer of food. As soon as the housekeeper left the kitchen, Chelsea plunged right in. 'Daddy, I have to talk to you.'

Her hopes rose as he folded his paper. 'Not now, Princess. I want to be at the bank by eight. Later, huh?' He ruffled her hair, just as he always had, absent-mindedly. He might just as well have been patting a dog, a puppy dog at that! At the door, he turned, frowning as though he'd just realised something. 'You'd better go shopping today, unless you've brought some nice dresses with you?'

She hadn't. Holidays were times when one didn't have to conform in any way, didn't have to wear any kind of uniform or 'appropriate' attire. Her case was stuffed with jeans, blouses, a couple of tracksuits and some underwear.

She spent the entire morning in Central Park, sitting on a bench and watching some children at play. At a little before noon she shoved her hands deep into the pockets of her denim jacket and walked some more—heading nowhere in particular—her head bent, shoulders hunched, spirits low. It was a crisp, early April day, not exactly cold, but the sky was clear and it wasn't warm enough for sitting on a park bench, motionless for hours, which she had been doing. She felt cold. She wished she'd brought a full-length coat. Maybe she should go and buy one? And a dress or two?

But she was in no mood for shopping. For what, anyhow? To please her father? Why should she dress up to please him when he never went out of his way to do anything for her, not even to listen to her these days. She would make him listen soon, though, she would make him understand how serious she was about not continuing her education.

When she got back to the apartment, however, she was told by Mrs Freer that her father had called to say he'd be late home, was not to be expected before ten. He was sorry, but ... it was business ...

By nine o'clock Chelsea was asleep, unable to keep her eyes open a minute longer. The rewards of jet-lag were not new to her.

The first few hours of the plane journey to Madrid passed in almost total silence. The day had started with an argument before Chelsea and her father left the apartment. Why hadn't she shopped for something decent to wear? he'd wanted to know. How could she think of travelling with him, first-class, dressed the way she was? Wasn't it high time she started paying attention to her appearance, her *grooming*, like other girls her age? What did they teach you at these English schools, for heaven's sake? To go around looking like a beatnik? (Chelsea had wanted to smile at the word, the out-dated concept, but hadn't dared.)

She glanced at her father now, a feeling of complete and utter frustration keeping her silent. She was so angry inside that she didn't trust herself to speak. Not here, in public, when even the cabin crew would hear her let rip, if she even ventured on to the subject of education.

Over the PA system came the sound of the captain's voice giving a report on the plane's whereabouts. Chelsea shifted her eyes back to the book on her lap. She hadn't turned a page in over an hour. When a smiling stewardess came and asked whether they'd care for any more drinks, Chelsea shook her head. Hal didn't even look up. He was reading papers he'd taken from his briefcase.

It had all gone so totally wrong. The argument that morning had prohibited the quiet and sensible conversation with him that she had rehearsed so well. Instead she had blurted it out to him, that she had no intention of going to finishing school next autumn. Worse, she had picked a moment when she was wide open for defeat.

His displeasure at her appearance had been followed by, 'I sincerely hope they'll do better with you at this finishing school, Chelsea. I don't know what's come over you these days. You used to be dressed like a little doll. I can only suppose you're going through——'

'Going through what?' she'd retorted. 'What would you know about what I'm going through? Well, I've got news for you, Daddy, I am not going to Switzerland. To that school or any other. Nor am I going to university. I've told Mother, now I'm telling you.'

'Aah!' He'd smiled then. 'So that's what it's about! Oh, your mother's told me all about it.'

Chelsea groaned and sank into a chair. She might have known! 'When did she call you? I take it she told you about our fight.'

'Of course.' He made a valiant effort to look concerned while at the same time overriding all her thoughts and feelings and ideas before she could even express them. 'She called me a couple of hours before you got into New York. She was upset, Chelsea. She said you'd spoken to her in a way that you've never spoken to her before. She was upset and angry.'

'That makes two of us.'

'Now listen.' He sat, his tone one of utter reasonableness as he spoke. 'You're tired. You've been doing a lot of studying, a lot of worrying. All you want is to get these examinations out of the way, I understand that. Do you think I never went through the phase you're experiencing now? We all go through it. Believe me, this is quite the wrong time to make decisions. Wait till the summer, you'll see things in an entirely different light.'

'But——'

'Do this for me, Princess,' he was cajoling then. And she had let him get away with it, had backed down because the car had arrived to take them to the airport.

And now, on the journey to Spain, she cursed herself for her own volatility. If she had only kept quiet that morning, they could be having an adult-to-adult discussion right now about her future. This would have been the perfect opportunity, while she had her father all to herself on this long and impossibly boring journey. But as things were, silence reigned, because as yet she was too angry to speak, and he was lost in his work.

There was no excitement for her, no sense of anticipation when they were finally coming in to land at Barajas Airport in Madrid. For one thing, she had lost interest in the trip and for another it was pitch dark outside and all she could see was a widespread haze of lights.

Being here was going to play havoc with her newly made adjustment to time again. Between Spain and England there was only an hour's difference in time, and it was her father who mentioned this, asking her whether she'd put her watch right. 'It's ten after ten here, precisely. Are you fit, Chelsea?'

She merely nodded. She was fit. Curiously enough, she was wide awake, a little stiff from the journey, but very much awake.

They sailed through passport control and customs. There was no need to ask whether they would be met. Where her father was, a chauffeur was never far away.

Chelsea didn't spot their driver. First the airport was quite busy and people were milling about, second, she was keeping an eye out for a man in uniform—or at least someone who would be holding a sign with the name Hal Prescott written on it. Instead, she heard a deep voice call her father's name and she looked around to see a tall man walking briskly towards them.

Without a glance in her direction, the man put both hands on her father's shoulders and squeezed hard, gripping his hand in a firm shake seconds later. Silent, standing still, Chelsea weighed the man up. He was smiling at Hal with the warmth and enthusiasm of a friend. No driver, this. This had to be their host, or at least one of the Colchero family. There was something about his bearing which spoke of pride, dignity, maybe even arrogance. His clothes, shoes, spoke for themselves. They were immaculate, smart, expensive, Yet when Chelsea's eyes travelled to his face, taking in the olive-coloured skin and the jet black hair, only one word sprang into her mind. *Gypsy*!

He looked like . . . like a . . . was there such a thing as a gypsy nobleman? Was his hair really that curly, naturally? Was it really so intensely black? Or was it just that she was seeing it in contrast with her father's hair, which was straight and dark blond?

For the moment, she was invisible. The two men were talking in English (her father's Spanish was not good), and she was able to assess the Spaniard without his knowing it. As tall as her father, who was six feet one according to his passport, the man was of a similar build, broad-shouldered and solid but slim. He was not young, he wasn't as old as Hal but he must have been thirty if he were a day . . .

And then his eyes turned their attention to her and she felt instantly uncomfortable. Blackness. She was being surveyed by pools of blackness which seemed in a mere glance to take in every hair on her head.

'My daughter,' Hal was saying, 'Chelsea. Darling, this is Señor Ricardo Juan Antonio Colchero de Castilla.'

There was thunderous laughter from the Spaniard as he reached for the hand she had automatically held out to him. 'Ricardo,' he amended. 'To you, *Ricardo*.' He gave her a slight bow and flashed her what he obviously thought was a winning smile, which she instantly disliked him for. She thought him a creep.

'*Señor*.' She withdrew her hand and looked down at

the floor. He was too much. Overbearing! And why were they standing around?

A moment later they were on their way. The driver had been there all the time, standing back while the greeting took place, and now he stepped forward to take the luggage and lead the way to Señor Colchero's car.

So this was Ramón's son. The elder of the two. Chelsea hoped that the younger son would be an improvement and that the girl, Mercedes, would be a vast improvement.

CHAPTER TWO

SHE was wishing she hadn't come. As they drove towards the centre of Madrid on the Spanish equivalent of a motorway, there was nothing to be seen but blackness to the left and the right, punctuated only occasionally by lights, a building.

Chelsea hadn't identified the make of the car they were in. It was dark and large, that's all she knew, large enough to accommodate all three of them comfortably on the back seat—though there were two other seats in front of them which would have pulled down. As it was they were sitting in a row with Hal in the middle. They'd driven just a few miles from the airport when Ricardo Colchero leaned forward to speak to her. 'So this is your first time in Spain, Chelsea?'

'That's right.'

'Well, we'll have to make it worthwhile for you. There's plenty that will interest you in Madrid, I'm sure.'

'I'm sure.' But she wasn't. There was probably nothing that would interest her in Madrid. Except the Prado Museum. That was one place she was hoping to get a look at.

'You're the same age as my sister. Did Hal tell you that?'

'Yes, *señor*, he did.' Polite, she had better be polite, though she was in no mood for small-talk. But she daren't let her father down, he was angry enough with her as it was. 'I look forward to meeting her.'

'Ricardo,' he corrected. 'Please.'

She inclined her head slightly, smiled slightly, then turned to look out of the window. A moment later she felt curiously compelled to look back at him and she found that his eyes were still upon her. Eyes that were interested in her, it seemed, eyes that were not too pleased with what they saw. For just a few seconds he held her gaze and then he dismissed her by addressing her father.

Chelsea's discomfort increased. What a creep! And yes, she'd been right in her very first impression. He was arrogant. She had cut short his small-talk and he hadn't liked that. But she hadn't been rude, so what the hell?

Madrid's city centre was far more interesting. The streets were wide, more like American boulevards. Different from London. For one thing, the pavements were lined with trees, she could see a long line of them ahead every time they turned a corner, The city was busy, too, with no shortage of people or traffic, shops, lights.

But that was all she got, impressions. She began, however, to look forward to seeing Madrid by daylight.

When the car drew to a halt outside a tall pair of wrought-iron gates, flanked on either side by high walls, Chelsea was surprised. They seemed to be right in the heart of town and this didn't look like a residential area. The driver got out of the car and opened the gates, slid back behind the wheel and moved the car on about fifty yards or so to the front door of a house which at first glance didn't seem at all splendid.

It was, though. It was bigger than it appeared to be on the outside, with a wide entrance hall which had a pink and grey marble floor. As they were ushered by Ricardo to the main salon they passed four Italian marble statues which Chelsea wanted to examine more closely. She would, but not now, not when her host was around.

She supposed the drawing room was typically Spanish. Whatever, she liked it. Many of its contents were old, very old probably, the paintings, the tapestries, the rugs. The furniture looked extremely comfortable, it was large and yet it managed also to be elegant. She liked the room.

Their suitcases had been whisked upstairs, a maid was waiting to take their coats and Ricardo was asking what they would like to drink. This, when from a door at the far end of the room there appeared a young girl with smiling eyes and a vivacious face and, most striking of all, a heavy mane of black hair which hung in waves down her back. It reached beyond her waist

Mercedes Colchero greeted Chelsea and her father as if she knew them both very well, which wasn't the case even with Hal, as far as Chelsea knew. She was dressed sombrely but immaculately and her manners were impeccable. Chelsea found herself assessing the girl as closely as she'd assessed her brother. The two girls were the same age, the same height and of a very similar build, though Chelsea was thinner.

Mercedes set about playing hostess to her guests and within half an hour the newcomers had been asked about their journey, given sandwiches (which was all they wanted), coffee and much polite chit-chat. Chelsea said very little. She observed that Mercedes' English was nowhere near as good as her brother's. His was almost faultless though quite heavily accented. And Mercedes seemed to be trying too hard somehow. Chelsea found it difficult to define quite what was wrong, quite why it was that she didn't take to the girl. She was certainly pleasant and friendly in a quiet yet smiling sort of way. Or maybe it was just that she looked so fresh and pretty—while Chelsea had to admit that she looked nothing short of scruffy herself. She was crumpled, and somehow or other she'd managed to get a streak of dirt down the left leg of her jeans. It looked black and awful against the pale blue.

'A drink, Hal?' Ricardo asked when a maid suddenly appeared as if from nowhere. 'Bourbon? Scotch?'

'Bourbon. Just as it comes.' Hal was obviously completely at home here.

'Now, I will call this a night.' Mercedes looked around, smiling.

'*It* a night, *niña*.' Big brother corrected her attempt at the English idiom, granted her that flashing smile of his and then turned to look at Chelsea. 'No doubt you would like to be shown to your room, too.' He turned away with, 'Mercedes will look after you.'

Chelsea had no doubt that Mercedes would. Perfectly, faultlessly. But she wasn't ready to go to bed yet—not when the idea had been presented to her almost as an order! So she put on her own flashing smile and aimed it straight at her host. 'Actually, no, *señor*, I'm far from tired. Perhaps I could have a glass of wine? That always makes me sleepy.'

Indeed? He didn't say the word, his eyebrows said it for him. Chelsea smiled inwardly, pleased with herself. She looked over at Mercedes, who was still seated, and caught something indefinable in her eyes. Whatever it was, it wasn't aimed at Chelsea, it was aimed at her brother. There seemed to be a question in her eyes.

'Good night, *niña*.' Ricardo answered the question, if that was what it was, with those three words.

The head of the household, *that's* what it was! Mercedes had silently asked her brother if she should stay around, because Chelsea was staying around. And big brother had told her she need not.

How pathetic, Chelsea thought. So much for modern Spain! Were Spanish attitudes just as they always had been? With the macho man and the obedient woman?

She went to bed an hour later and slept well, in a room which was comfortable and full of character. There was an adjoining bathroom and the maid had unpacked for her and turned down the bed. Chelsea flopped into it and slept like a log.

She woke early, drawing back the heavy curtains to see a bright blue cloudless sky. She showered, washed her short, curly hair and left it to dry naturally. After pulling on jeans and a lightweight sweater, she went downstairs. Although she had set her watch the previous night, she'd forgotten to wind it and had no idea of the time. A clock in the hall told her it was almost seven.

After examining the marble statues, she wandered around from room to room. In the dining room she was greeted by a young maid who was setting the table. Pointing the way, the girl informed her that Mercedes was up and could be found in the courtyard.

The house really was splendid, and enchanting. Chelsea hadn't seen anything like it before. She hadn't suspected it was built around a courtyard—but there it was, complete with a fountain, shrubs and tubs overflowing with brilliantly coloured flowers. Sitting on a small, stone bench nearby was Mercedes, seeming lost in her thoughts. She didn't hear Chelsea's approach and was staring down pensively at the cobblestones, unseeing.

Chelsea paused for a moment, watching her. Again she was dressed sombrely and while the dark colours matched her mood of the moment, they didn't seem right for the cheerful personality Chelsea had witnessed the previous night. And then she remembered. The girl was still in mourning; she had lost her father only three months earlier.

'Chelsea!' Mercedes was suddenly on her feet, startled. 'Good morning. You sleep well, I hope?' The brightness was back, the perfect young hostess was smiling again.

'Thanks, yes. I—I should have said this last night, Mercedes. I'm very sorry about—your father. I met him once, a few years ago. He was a nice man.'

'Thank you.' Her eyes were not as dark as her brother's. They were softer, too, dark brown and smiling now. 'As a matter of fact I was just thinking about him.'

'I'm sorry I disturbed you. I hadn't intended to get up this early!'

'Not at all! Come, let us have breakfast.' She linked her arm through Chelsea's, making her feel both pleased and awkward at the same time.

They had coffee and croissants in the dining room, and Mercedes apologised because she would have to leave her guest alone that morning. 'And my grandmother won't come downstairs until about ten o'clock, I'm afraid. But I'll be back for lunch and then we'll go out and I'll show you something of our city. I have an English lesson, you see.'

'An English lesson?'

Mercedes' smile was almost sad then. 'I know. My English should be better than it is. My French isn't all that good, either. Ricardo is not pleased.'

What possible difference could it make to her brother? But Chelsea said nothing. Instead she asked about the other, younger brother. 'Doesn't he come home during the holidays? Which university is he at?'

'Not always. He will come home in the summer. He's in England, at Oxford.' The last word was spoken with pride. 'Vincente is very clever. Not as clever as Ricardo, of course, but I'm the . . . what's the word? The slow one in the family?'

'The word you're looking for is "dunce". But I'm sure that isn't true!'

Mercedes shrugged, not at all sure about that. 'Anyway, I'm sorry I have to leave you alone for a while.' She was frowning.

'Don't be. I'm very good at entertaining myself.'

Mercedes' frown only deepened. 'You see, I didn't until yesterday know you were coming here—that your father was taking you here, I mean. And on Friday I'm going to a wedding and——'

'Please!' Chelsea laughed at her. 'Will you stop worrying? I've told you, I'm very happy on my own. I'm a loner, always have been.'

'A loner? What is that?'

'It means I'm happy with my own company. Not all the time, of course, but I can certainly amuse myself for the day while you're at this wedding. Anyhow, we might be gone by then. I just don't know yet. But don't worry.' The girl's fussing was beginning to irritate. It was so obvious that the two of them had nothing in common, Chelsea didn't want to be tied to her in any case. She wanted to explore the city on her own.

But they did have one thing in common. It was Mercedes who mentioned it. 'I understand we're going—we will be going—to the same school in Switzerland later this year. I haven't been in Switzerland more than once. Have you?'

'No.' Chelsea's answer came sharply. She leaned forward, making her point with sudden forcefulness. 'I haven't been there at all. And you won't be seeing me there!'

Mercedes simply didn't understand that remark. 'It is—how do you call it? A co— ... Chelsea?' She appealed for help.

'Coincidence.' Having supplied the word in English, Chelsea went on to repeat it in Spanish. And she spoke in Spanish throughout the ensuing conversation, wanting no more misunderstandings. She saw Mercedes' look of surprise, followed by one of astonishment. 'It's no coincidence. It seems that your father recommended the school to my father. My mother, however, had already decided that that's where I should go to be— "finished". *Finished!* What does it mean? Well, I'm telling you this, I'm not going there!'

The Spanish girl looked amazed. 'You don't want to?'

'Too right!'

'But your father——'

'My father will be made to understand.' A little of her force vanished then and she shifted in her seat, hoping she was right. 'Just as soon as I can get a chance to talk to him . . .'

'But it's such a wonderful school, such a wonderful opportunity!'

'*Opportunity?* For what? To learn how to walk with a pile of books balanced on your head? To learn how to arrange flowers for dinner tables? To learn how to address a—an ambassador or something?'

'Well, yes! All of that.' Mercedes was as puzzled as Chelsea was cross.

'And what the hell do you want to know all that for? How will you ever put it to use?'

'In my marriage, of course.'

'In your *marriage*?' Chelsea was appalled. 'You certainly believe in looking ahead, don't you?'

Still her sarcasm went over the other girl's head. 'Looking ahead? But, Chelsea, I am betrothed. Soon I'll be getting engaged.'

'Betrothed!' Dear God, what kind of word was that? The idea of it! 'What do you mean, "betrothed"? Don't tell me you were assigned to someone while you were still in your cradle?'

'What?'

'I said, are you telling me your family have *arranged* a marriage for you?'

As if she suddenly understood, Mercedes smiled. 'No, no. But as it happens, this is a boy I've known all my life.'

'And you're going to tell me he's from a very good family.'

'Of course he is. I—I don't understand you.'

Chelsea sighed in exasperation. 'Never mind. Go on, tell me.'

Although they were speaking in Spanish, they might just as well have been talking in different languages. The girls' thinking was divergent, to say the least.

Mercedes' smile widened. It was all so straightforward to her. 'I suppose our families assumed Emilio and I would marry, but they never put any pressure on us. None at all,' she added defensively. 'We're in love. It's as simple as that.'

'Sure. And what does he do, this Emilio? Will I get to meet him?'

'I'm afraid not. He's doing his National Service.'

'And how long does that last?'

'A year.'

'And then what?'

'Then we get officially engaged. He—I—Ricardo suggested I wait until Emilio had finished in the army, until I was a little older. He's nineteen. But we won't marry until he's completed his education. That will be two years later and——'

In a rush of non-comprehending annoyance, Chelsea slammed a hand against the table. 'You make it sound so cut and dried! How much thinking have you done for yourself? That's what I'd like to know!'

'But, Chelsea . . .' Mercedes was looking positively upset. 'It's been understood for a long time that Emilio and I would marry!'

'Exactly!' Chelsea muttered aloud in English, just a few unladylike words which the other girl wouldn't understand. 'My God, how can you let them all *control* you like that?'

'But it's what I want!'

'Rubbish! It's what you've been brought up to think you want! I tell you, *I've* decided for myself, about *my* life. There's no way I'm going to finishing school, there's no way I'll ever marry. As for the idea of having children, well, that's one nuisance in life I can happily live without! I suppose *you'll* take them for granted and be expected to have a houseful. For heaven's sake, Mercedes, haven't you stopped to think you might have been conditioned, pre-programmed?'

There was silence. Complete stillness. Mercedes was looking at her as though she were of a different species.

Then there was a voice, a deep voice which shattered the silence and came as a shock to both girls. 'Why don't you answer the question, Mercedes?'

Chelsea spun round in her chair, aghast. Ricardo Colchero was leaning against the door-jamb, appearing amused and relaxed, as though he'd been there a long time. He looked just as immaculate as he had the night before, dressed in a dark business suit and an impossibly white shirt. He had what the Spanish call 'casta', a certain dignity, almost an arrogance about his bearing. 'How much have you heard, señor?'

He moved into the room, answering her demand calmly. 'I heard all of it, Chelsea. I stood and I listened. And very interesting it was.'

He ignored her scowl. He sat down at the head of the table, between the two girls. 'So, niña?' He looked straight at his sister. 'Answer the question.'

Mercedes didn't seem so sure of herself now. 'Well, yes, I suppose ... I suppose my grandmother and my father ... maybe I was brought up to ... But this is what I want.' She asserted herself, shaking her head as though Chelsea had put in it something which shouldn't be there. She looked Chelsea straight in the eye. 'You're wrong. This is what I want. I want to be married, to Emilio. And yes, I want children. Two, three, six of them! And what's wrong with that?' She asked this question gently, searching Chelsea's eyes for some hint of understanding.

Ricardo looked at her with unconcealed amusement. 'Over to you, I believe.'

Chelsea put both hands flat on the table. 'Nothing. Nothing at all. For some people. I'm not picking a fight.' That sentence was aimed at Ricardo. 'Our conversation was not intended for your entertainment, señor, or for your ears. So I'll finish by saying there's nothing wrong with what your sister wants—provided she's sure it's what she wants and it's not the result of pressure from others.'

Ricardo inclined his head. 'Mercedes, could it be that? Please think about it.'

She did, for a moment. She still looked vaguely upset. 'No. It's what I want.'

There followed a silence during which Chelsea felt extremely ill at ease. She was just about to excuse herself, when Ricardo looked at his watch. 'Mercedes, you have things to discuss with the housekeeper before you leave for your lesson.'

'*Si*, Ricardo.' Mercedes got up. Her smile was back as she looked at their guest—probably because she felt it ought to be. 'I'll see you at lunch time, Chelsea.'

Chelsea found herself alone with the man then, which was the last thing she wanted. 'Well, er, I think I'll go——'

'Stay. I want to talk to you.'

She groaned inwardly. If he thought he could play the heavy-handed chauvinist with her, he was wrong. 'I don't think you and I have anything to say to each other, *señor*.' She got to her feet only to find that his fingers suddenly closed around her wrist. His grip was just a little too tight and it irritated her. But she sat. Why, she wasn't sure, exactly. She told herself it was for the sake of peace.

So she sat down again and Ricardo looked at her. He just looked, with a great deal of curiosity, for what seemed like minutes.

'Well?' she demanded at length. 'Why are you looking at me like that?'

He didn't answer her question. He asked several of his own. 'Why are you so angry, so aggressive? About what are you so disturbed? And why this jaundiced view of marriage? This, at eighteen years of age.'

Stupidly, she corrected him. 'Seventeen.' More stupidly she added, 'I'm—nearly eighteen. I—I'll be eighteen at the end of May.' She was blushing furiously now with embarrassment.

'Next month? So there's just two months' difference between you and my sister. Yet you are so much less mature.'

Her head came up in defiance. 'On the contrary, *I've* learned to think for myself!'

Indeed? Again, his expression said it for him. Those gypsy-like features had a way of talking without the necessity for words. She didn't think him a good-looking man. He was . . . too intense. Everything about his features was too intense.

He considered her, remaining quiet for several seconds. 'So you know who you are and what you want in life?'

'Yes!' No. Inwardly, she was deflated because in fact she didn't know either of those things. She didn't really understand why she was so angry at life, at the world. She didn't know what she wanted from life. She didn't even know whether she was American or English, whether she was still a child or whether she was an adult.

Ricardo leaned forward slightly, his black eyes looking straight into hers. Quietly he said, 'Be careful about what you want, *niña*, because that's surely what you'll get.'

Her eyebrows were drawn together, her eyes narrowed as she was trapped in his gaze. She thought about his statement and could make no sense of it. All that really registered was one word. She looked away, shrugging, frowning. 'Don't call me that.'

'*Niña?*'

Girl child. Little girl. 'Yes, I don't like it. Especially coming from you.'

There was silence again. Chelsea started to get up but again his hand snaked out and circled her wrist. 'Not yet, *niña*, not yet.'

She tried to pull her hand away but his fingers only tightened, his arm coming out to accommodate her movement. He didn't even budge in his seat.

She sat, cursing herself for doing so. She was responding to him like Mercedes did, obeying him. But she was doing it only to keep the peace. After all, she was a guest in his house and if she told this man what she thought of him, that she considered him nothing more than an autocratic bully, she'd have her father to contend with. 'Where's my father?'

'He's looking over some papers in my study, he'll be in shortly. So?'

'So—what?'

'You were about to tell me what you want from life.'

'I . . . not a lot,' she said sullenly. Then, positively because it was the truth, 'I want to travel. I want—for heaven's sake, I want to *live*!'

His surveillance continued in another silence, an awkward one for Chelsea, who wished she'd kept her big mouth shut. Why was she suffering from such lack of control these days? Such outbursts?

'To live.' He said at length, thoughtful. 'To travel. Is that why you don't want to go to the finishing school?'

She gasped. 'You heard all that?'

'I told you, I heard the entire conversation.'

'I——' She hardly knew what to say. He was irritating her beyond words, the way he was watching her, weighing every syllable she uttered. She had to get away, 'Please, *señor*——'

'Ricardo.'

'Ricardo. All right, all right. I—I'd be obliged if you don't say anything to my father. I haven't had a chance to discuss it with him yet . . . not properly.'

'I wouldn't dream of it.' He seemed very serious.

She looked at him uncertainly. 'May I go now?'

He held up his hands in a wide gesture. 'But of course! There's just one more thing—your father and I will be leaving for the bank in an hour or so. Tell me, how are you going to amuse yourself till lunch time?'

'Easily.' Chelsea got up quickly. Somehow he managed to make her feel gauche, foolish, irritated. She was also a little bemused by him. He was a strange man, very strange. As she reached the door, she heard her name being spoken very quietly and she turned, frowning. 'Yes?'

'Do you find it so difficult,' he asked, still in that extremely quiet voice, 'to have a conversation with me?'

'Frankly,' she said, 'yes.'

Her first day in Madrid was most enjoyable. She honestly didn't intend to stay out all day, just till lunch time. She left the house after getting her jacket from her bedroom, alone and unnoticed, and she walked until she spotted a hotel. She went up to the concierge and asked him if he could give her a map of the city, which he did, happily. He probably thought she was staying there. She opened the map and asked him to point out exactly where she was.

'Here,' he smiled. 'You are in the area known as Barrio de Salamanca. 'Exactly here.' He pinpointed a place on the map 'We're in la Calle de Goya.'

La Calle de Goya. How charming! A street named after the artist. 'And the Museo del Prado? Where is that? Is it within walking distance?'

The middle-aged man looked her over, his smile broadening. 'For you, yes. For me, it would be a taxi ride.'

She thanked him and made her way, reading the map easily. Madrid was very logically set out, not quite as simply as New York, but she would have no problem finding her way around.

The trouble was that she didn't go straight to the Museum. She took a short cut through El Retiro, the huge park right in the heart of the city, and there was so much going on there, it was an entertainment in itself.

The sun was shining and it had brought all sorts of people out of the woodwork. There were people selling their wares, jewellery, paintings, sketches, jumping beans, anything and everything. There were people boating on the lake, people standing in groups, talking, smoking, having a drink at the open-air café. There were lots of children around, some carrying balloons, some squabbling with each other, chasing each other, some feeding the fish in the lake.

The trees were out in all their spring glory, hundreds and hundreds of them. Odd characters were sitting on benches or on the grass, and at one point she saw a fortune-teller, crystal ball and all, who had quite a crowd around her. Obviously her customer had no objection to the rest of the world hearing what life had in store for him.

There was so much to take in, so many colours, smells, sights, sounds and the exciting air of—of *foreignness*. Chelsea loved the place. It was a huge park and she didn't cover all of it by any means. She stopped to rest near a fountain, chatted to an old lady who was dressed entirely in black and carrying a shopping bag which was empty but for a rolled-up blanket. At least, that's what she thought it was. It was some time before she realised there was a mangy-looking cat wrapped up in the blanket. She laughed, gave the old lady the price of a meal when asked for the price of a cup of coffee, and finally moved on in the direction of the café, realising how hungry she was herself. It was some later that she got to the Prado.

She spent the entire afternoon in there. The Museum was one place which didn't close for siesta. Even so it wasn't long enough, and when she looked at her watch—finally—and realised it was almost five o'clock, she knew she would have to come back another time. The works of Goya, Velázquez and El Greco, among many others, took time to study. And Chelsea was fascinated by them.

She took a taxi back to the Colchero house and was met by Mercedes almost before she got through the front door.

'I'm sorry, I——' Chelsea started to apologise, was about to explain that she'd got carried away with her sightseeing, but Mercedes stuck a finger over her lips and ushered her into a small sitting room off to the right. She looked almost frantic and Chelsea was at a loss to understand why.

'What's up? What's wrong? I've said I'm sorry and——'

'It's your father.' Mercedes' hands were moving about expressively, quickly. 'He said he wants to see you immediately you come in. So does my brother.

They're angry with you, especially Ricardo. You'd better apologise to him.' She was babbling away in rapid Spanish.

'To your brother? But why? What——'

'*Please*, Chelsea, you must do this! You shouldn't speak to Ricardo the way you do.'

'I don't know what you mean.' Letting out a bored breath, she went on, 'Look, just because you're scared of the man doesn't mean that I have to be.'

'Scared of him? I'm not scared of him.' It was as if Mercedes didn't know what to do with her guest then. She looked helpless. 'I—oh you don't understand! Ricardo isn't a person to be afraid of, but you—the way you spoke to him this morning, I—it wasn't right. I was afraid for *you*. My brother is as kind and as loving as my father was, but he also has my father's temper . . .' She left the warning hanging in the air.

Chelsea was nonplussed. Kind? Loving? Temper? What was the girl talking about? 'Where are they?' she demanded. She would sort this out herself. 'Your brother, my father?'

'They're in Ricardo's study. Chelsea——'

But Chelsea had already gone. She tapped briskly on the study door and walked in confidently, not waiting for an answer. 'So what's all the fuss about?' She aimed the words at the room in general, before she had time to take in the men's faces. When she saw the expression her father was wearing, however, it took the wind out of her sails. He was livid, she'd never seen him look like that before. Never.

'So you're back!' He viciously stubbed out the cigar he was smoking and stood, his face flushed with anger. 'Chelsea, you'll apologise to Ricardo at once, and make it good! Where the devil have been been? How dare you behave like this when you're a guest in someone's house? Who gave you permission to go roaming the streets of a strange city, alone? Are you crazy or something?'

He gave her no chance to answer, to apologise, to anything. She just stood there, open-mouthed, her face getting redder and redder. She'd never seen him so angry! And it was all over nothing!

Ricardo was sitting behind a large, leather-topped desk. He spoke in the midst of Hal's tirade, just one word, 'Hal——'

'That's okay, Ricardo.' Her father's hand came up as if to pacify the Spaniard. 'I'll deal with this.' He never took his eyes from his daughter, nor she from him, but she was acutely aware of Ricardo's presence and the humiliation he was witnessing. 'Chelsea, I don't know what's got into you lately but I don't like it, that's for sure. Last fall you were a regular kind of girl, the next thing I know, at Christmas, you're as awkward as the devil. You dress like a vagabond, you have no sense of responsibility, and now this! I don't understand you any more——'

He never had. That was the trouble. 'Daddy, I'm seventeen years old! I'm a New Yorker! Why you were worried about me exploring this city, I can't imagine! But that isn't what it's about, is it? Not really. It's him. You're angry because I've upset *him*!' She pointed to Ricardo without looking at him. She was too embarrassed to look at him, and in that instant she hated both men with a ferocity that almost choked her. She was very near to tears—but she was damned if she'd cry!

'Hal——' The word came again from Ricardo.

Hal turned to him. 'You've got it,' he said. He turned back to his daughter, glaring at her. 'Apologise. And make it good!'

It was more than she could tolerate. Her chin came up even as her eyes turned dangerously brighter. It was on the tip of her tongue to tell her father to get lost ... but she couldn't do it. Besides, it would be wrong to do it in front of the Spaniard, she knew that. But she couldn't apologise, either. Not at that instant. She found that she couldn't speak at all, not without crying, and she wasn't going to do that.

The result was an awful, horrible deadlock as father and daughter faced one another. Again, Chelsea backed down, was the first to look away, but the silence was broken by Ricardo.

He got to his feet. 'Hal, I'd like to talk to your daughter alone. Would you mind?'

This seemed to satisfy the older man enormously. He nodded, almost smiling. 'Be my guest.' He walked to the door. 'She's all yours, and if you feel like giving her the spanking I should have given her months ago, feel free.' He slammed the door behind him and Chelsea spun round to face the man who was moving towards her.

Heavens, he wasn't going to try it, was he? From the look on his face, she wouldn't put it past him! 'Don't touch me!'

'Be quiet.' He had almost reached her now, but this time she would not back down. Not from him. She stuck her hands on her hips and glared at him defiantly, her cheeks burning with humiliation. 'Get away from me!'

Ricardo glanced heavenward and let out a weary breath. 'Sit down, *niña*, and tell me——'

If he hadn't taken hold of her arm, she wouldn't have reacted the way she did, but in her haze of anger she misunderstood his action, didn't even hear what he was asking her to do. As it was, she wrenched her left arm from his grip and brought her right hand up in an effort to fight him off. He seemed both surprised and amused as he easily caught hold of her wrist in mid air. 'Will you please calm down——'

'Let go of me!' The resentment which burst from her was far more than that which she felt towards the Spaniard; it was a resentment which had been simmering in her for weeks, months, probably even for years. Nobody was interested in her, nobody would

listen to her point of view over any matter—even the
one that was causing this trouble. 'I'm sick of being
dictated to! I'm a free person and I'll do with myself as
I please!'

'That's fine by me.' Ricardo's reply was calm but it was
she who wasn't listening now. He still had hold of her
wrist but he made the mistake of slackening his grip.

'I said let *go* of me!' She screamed at him and at the
same time yanked her arm free ... and this time she
succeeded in slapping him.

Something changed dramatically in his face, his eyes
were suddenly darker than ever as he stared down at
her. She'd gone too far, much too far, and she knew it.
She could feel the blood draining from her face, could
almost hear the tension in the silence between them.

If she could have seen her own face, if she could have
seen the fear in her eyes, she'd have understood why
Ricardo managed to keep control of himself. And he
did. He merely lifted her by her upper arms, clean off
the floor, and deposited her on to the leather armchair
facing his desk—just as though she were nothing more
than an overgrown doll.

Stunned by his action, his strength, she felt the blood
rushing back to her cheeks and she stared helplessly at
the carpet, hardly able to breathe.

Neither of them moved, neither of them spoke. After
a few seconds Ricardo shoved his hands into the
pockets of his trousers and moved over to the window,
turning his back to her. When she heard the quiet, 'Stay
where you are, Chelsea,' she did so. There was no
escape. She might just as well live through the rest of
her humiliation. In the long run, it would be the
quickest way of getting out of this room.

Long minutes passed during which she braced herself
for another verbal onslaught. At length she was able to
look at him but he still had his back to her, was looking
out of the window, motionless, standing easy, relaxed,
leaning with one shoulder against the wall.

After a few more silent minutes, she actually felt herself relaxing a little, becoming composed. She would be able to cope now.

But nothing was happening, nothing was being said . . .

He turned once to look at her and she stared at him curiously, at a loss to understand this silence. He turned back to the window.

Ricardo left the girl in peace. She'd had enough. He wasn't sure yet how he would handle this, but it certainly wouldn't be in the manner in which Hal had handled it. Hal Prescott might be an extremely clever man as far as finance was concerned but he didn't use his brains when it came to handling his daughter. She was so insecure, he could almost see the word written on her forehead. She was frightened, too, not just now, but generally. It was in her eyes almost constantly. She was so painfully young and confused. He found himself thinking of his own father with gratitude. Not that that was anything new.

When he felt sure she'd had time to calm down, when he knew he could spare her the humiliation of her tears, when he knew what tactics to use, he said, 'You may go now, Chelsea.'

He spoke in Spanish and she thought she had misunderstood or misheard him . . . and yet she knew she had not. 'What?'

'You may go. Dinner's at eight-thirty. My uncles are joining us, with their wives. Some of my cousins will be coming with them. They're nice people, all of them.'

'I—oh.' She was fazed, totally fazed. 'I—I'm——'

'Yes?' He turned then, a smile on his face, as though she'd just asked him whether he'd like to hear a joke.

There was suspicion stamped all over her features. 'What's wrong?' He spoke gently and as if he didn't understand her at all.

'Well, I—nothing.' She slumped back in the chair. For a few seconds, she said nothing. Then, confusedly,

'I mean, er, I didn't expect ... I thought you were angry with me?'

'How come your Spanish is so good?'

She was almost tongue-tied now. She couldn't understand the man at all. Not one little bit. 'My— Spanish?' When he nodded, she said, 'They—they tell me I have a gift for languages.'

'It's more than that. Your Spanish isn't solely from textbooks.' And then he smiled. So did she, she smiled because she simply couldn't help it.

'Okay, I'll come clean. My best friend in school is Latin American. Her father is working in England and she's been attending my school for the past two years. She's from Venezuela, actually.'

'Really?' Ricardo immediately went into the differences between the accents, the different meanings of some of the words used in Latin America and in Spain.

Chelsea suddenly found herself talking easily with him, telling him about her Spanish teacher, Sister Teresa, and how she was unlikely to get confused between her teaching and Carmen Romero's extra-curricular lessons—in other words, Carmen's chatting. 'It's all very interesting, you see. Carmen talks to me in Spanish most of the time but Sister Teresa puts me straight if I wander from the Castillian accent.'

'Your accent is very good.'

'Thank you. So's yours.'

He looked dubious. 'My English accent?'

'No, your Spanish accent. Your English accent is *awful!*

'Thank you!'

It was only when she became conscious of the fact that she was laughing with him that she sobered. 'I— I'm sorry about today, Ricardo. The truth is I got carried away.'

He was quiet for a moment, serious now, but Chelsea found she could take his criticism when it came. 'You worried us, all of us. And Doña Teodora, my grandmother, was looking forward to meeting you at lunch time. It was thoughtless of you not to let anyone know where you were going, when you'd be back.'

'Yes, I—I suppose it was. I apologise.'

'*Muy bien.* And where did you get to today? Anywhere interesting?'

She went into enthusiastic descriptions of El Retiro and the Prado, with Ricardo listening carefully.

'Chelsea——' He paused, musing over her name, and she smiled to herself because she wondered whether he was going to ask a question she'd been asked a hundred times before. He was. 'Chelsea? Isn't that the name of a district in London? Were you born there?'

'No. I was born in London but not in Chelsea.'

'Yet you referred to yourself earlier as a New Yorker. Is that how you see yourself?'

'I—not really.' That was the trouble. She didn't 'see' herself as anything in particular. 'I was taken to New York shortly after my birth and I spent seven years of my life there, but I've been educated mainly in England. I—I'm not really sure where I belong.'

'Tell me, where else have you been in the world? Apart from New York. And England, of course.'

'France. Once, just for two weeks. It was a trip from school.' He was looking at her expectantly and she shrugged. 'That's it. Nowhere else.'

He seemed surprised. 'What about holidays with your parents?'

'When my father has time, we go to his house in California. He has a beach house in Carmel.'

'And your mother?'

'She never has time to take me on holiday.'

Ricardo wanted to pursue that, but he didn't. Of itself the sentence told him a great deal, anyway. Instead he switched back to the subject which interested her most. 'And where would you like to go, especially? Which countries would you like to see?'

'All of them.'

Her answer came so seriously that he couldn't help smiling. 'That would take a very long time, *niña*.'

It didn't bother her then, the fact that he'd called her little girl. Maybe that's how he saw her. As he saw his sister. 'Ricardo, may I ask you—how old are you?'

'Oh, I'm quite ancient. Twenty-nine.'

She cocked her head to one side. 'I thought you were older.'

'Thank you again!'

'I'm sorry, I didn't mean to . . .' She started giggling when she saw the grin on his face. 'Have you done much travelling?'

'A great deal. And my work takes me all over the place.'

'It does?'

'You think I sit behind a desk all day?' He was laughing openly now. She thought he looked younger when he laughed. 'I leave that to my uncles. No, I'm the one who goes out chasing business. Are you really interested in what I do?'

'No,' she said, unthinking.

This was followed by thunderous laughter, just as she'd heard from him when she'd first met him at the airport, when her father had introduced him by his full and impressive name.

Chelsea watched him carefully, amused by his amusement. She did a slight revision of her opinion of him. He wasn't too bad, after all. At least he had a sense of humour, even if his laughter was at her expense!

'You are honest, little one, I must say that for you.' She had character, too. He could see in her the makings of a very interesting woman. But right now she was a pretty, skinny teenager who was lonely and very much in need of some understanding. And Hal was almost as confused as she was. There was obviously no room in his world for a teenage girl, rebellious or otherwise. He was out of his depth. 'Would you like to see more of the city tomorrow, Chelsea? With Mercedes,' he added pointedly.

'Very much!'

'Then I'll organise it. I'll make some suggestions and see that you have an interesting tour.'

Chelsea went back to her bedroom, where she found Mercedes waiting for her. She was sitting, looking tense, on a chair by the window. 'I hope you don't mind my waiting here for you,' she said apologetically, gesturing around her. 'I thought . . . Are you all right?'

Grinning, Chelsea told her to speak in English, that it would be good practice for her. 'Of course I'm all right.'

'But, Ricardo—was he very angry with you?'

'If he was, it didn't show. I saw nothing of the temper you spoke of.' Nor could she imagine that Ricardo's father had had a temper, either. She couldn't see any similarity at all between Ricardo and Ramón Colchero. Ricardo was very different from the teasing, jovial man she remembered. But there again, Ricardo no longer fitted the impression she'd had of him up until an hour ago. She found she no longer disliked him, though he was still difficult to understand . . .

'Your brother is a strange man,' she muttered.

Mercedes' mouth opened in protest but she didn't get a chance to speak. 'You might have told me there's to be a dinner party tonight,' Chelsea went on. 'I haven't got anything to wear. Except jeans, I mean.'

Mercedes was looking lost again, almost incredulous. 'You have no dresses with you?'

'Nope. Not one.'

'But——' Her hands fluttered about expressively but she failed miserably to express herself. 'Come to my room. I can find plenty of things for you. You ought——'

Chelsea clamped a hand on her shoulder. 'Wait a minute. I'm going to dress tonight because I *want* to, not because I *ought* to. Do you understand?'

'No,' came the simple reply.

CHAPTER THREE

'Do you understand?'

'No.'

At eleven-thirty the following day, the two girls looked at one another and, because it seemed there was nothing else they could do about the situation, they started laughing.

They were in a store called Galerías Preciados in La Calle de Serrano—the Bond Street of Madrid. For the past couple of hours Chelsea had been dragged from expensive shop to expensive shop, repeatedly rejecting Mercedes' suggestions of the clothes she should try on. Their ideas on what would suit Chelsea were different, to say the least. Still, she did have one full carrier bag to show for her efforts, which included a full-length coat.

The problem between the girls now was the chauffeur-driven car that had stalked them all morning, the car that went with the Colchero house. Mercedes gave up. 'All right, tell me how I'm supposed to show you the city if I dismiss the driver?'

'On foot?'

'On foot? And how many miles can you walk in an afternoon?'

'Okay, okay, point taken.' Chelsea was not enjoying herself. She didn't like shopping, she didn't like being chaperoned by a chauffeur and she didn't like the idea of being driven around in a car all afternoon, that was not her idea of exploring. 'Then we'll use the Metro.'

'The *Metro*?'

Chelsea blinked in surprise. 'Why not? I've got a map here and I can——'

'Are you teasing me, Chelsea?' Mercedes was looking bewildered again. 'I know what my father would have said about that idea. As for my grandmother—she'd have a fit at the very thought of it!'

'What? *Why?* Why should——' But the look on the other girl's face stopped her. Suddenly she understood. It wasn't done. It simply wasn't done for someone like Mercedes to travel on the Metro. Chelsea pitied her in that moment, realising that her new acquaintance had led a life which was even more sheltered than her own. Worse, Mercedes seemed to have no desire for—well, no sense of *adventure*.

Chelsea sighed, resigning herself. 'Perhaps you're right. Perhaps it would be more convenient to go by car.'

They had been back at the house for an hour that evening when a maid knocked on Chelsea's door and informed her that Señor Colchero wished to see her in his study. She went at once, wondering what she'd done wrong this time. She put the question to him as soon as she got through the door.

'Nothing at all . . . to my knowledge.' Ricardo was sitting at his desk. He wasn't smiling but his black eyes were glittering with amusement.

Chelsea sat down, relieved. 'I suppose Mercedes has already reported to you about our day?'

'No. I thought I'd ask you about that.'

So be it, she thought, plunging at once into a detailed diatribe of all they had done—and said. 'Well, we went shopping and we disagreed about everything I tried on. Then we had lunch and disagreed over whether it should be a meal or a snack. Then I wanted to get rid of the driver and walk around the city, or use the Metro, and Mercedes seemed to think I was off my head. Would you mind telling me why your sister is not allowed to use public transport? I don't understand her, or you, any more than either of you understand me.'

Ricardo considered her in silence, his face impassive. 'I understand you very well, *niña*. More than you realise. You and my sister are merely different

personalities, different people with different—histories.'
He had been going to say 'home lives' but thought
better of it. This child hadn't had a home life.

'Mercedes is a snob,' Chelsea said bluntly. 'But don't
misunderstand,' she added quickly, 'I don't dislike her.
We're at least learning to laugh about our differences.'

'That's healthy.' Ricardo had to suppress a smile.
Such sweeping statements she came out with! 'Chelsea,
all her life my sister has been surrounded by family, her
parents when they were alive, her brothers, uncles,
aunts, cousins. This is the Spanish way, though things
are changing. But changes come slowly. Of course her
grandmother would have a fit at the idea of her—and
you—roaming Madrid on the Metro. You are both
extremely young and naïve and pretty, all of which
makes you vulnerable. This is a big city and there are
certain quarters of it in which young girls simply would
not be safe to walk—especially rich young girls whose
family names are known throughout Spain. Do you
follow me?'

'I—do you mean she might get kidnapped or
something?'

His eyebrows rose slightly. 'Or something.'

'That's an awful penalty to pay for being rich! I
wouldn't know. I'm not rich. I mean, my family's not
rich in the same way yours is.' Nor, in her opinion, was
she pretty.

'Penalty? What is this penalty you speak of?'

'The lack of freedom, of course!'

'But my sister has all the freedom she wants.'

'She does not! She daren't even——'

'All the freedom *she wants*. Like I say, you and
Mercedes are different people. So tell me, what did you
see this afternoon?'

Chelsea was quiet for a moment, considering. He was
right, after all. Mercedes had not, in fact, wanted to go
on the Metro. She hadn't wanted to experience
something new. Still, while her outlook on life, her

attitudes towards it were very different from her own, Chelsea did privately envy her some of the things she had—like her warm and loving family, for instance. 'Mm? Oh, we saw the Royal Palace, The Plaza de España, the waxworks and—well, you know, you organised the tour. And it was all the tourist stuff!' she added disparagingly.

Ricardo Colchero leaned forward, resting his chin on his hands as he considered her. 'And the tourist stuff, as you put it, did not satisfy you? Didn't entertain you?'

'Well, yes. But what I really wanted to see . . .' She amended her words passionately. 'What I really want to see is the *guts* of Madrid!' She waited, then, for laughter, for a look of non-comprehension. Yet if Ricardo had asked her to define what she meant, she couldn't have. Before anything else could be said, however, the door opened and Chelsea's father walked in.

His eyes went straight to his daughter and then to the Spaniard. 'Anything wrong?'

'Nothing at all, Hal.' Ricardo got up and perched on the side of his desk. 'Chelsea was just telling me what a very successful day she's had.' He glanced down at her, caught her look of astonishment and gave her a quick, conspiratorial wink, unseen by her father.

She was even more confused by what came next. 'Since I won't be involved in your meeting tomorrow, Hal, I wonder whether I might take your daughter out for the day? My sister is going to a wedding out of town, which leaves Chelsea at a loose end.'

Hal was confused, too. 'Sure, but I don't want her being a nuisance. You don't have to entertain her!'

'On the contrary.' The Spaniard's reply was full of amusement. 'She is going to entertain me.' He turned to the dumbfounded seventeen-year-old, adding, 'Isn't that so, *niña*?'

* * *

'I feel as though I've walked for miles!'

Ricardo grinned. 'You have. *We* have.'

It was seven in the evening when they got back from their sightseeing the next day. It had been a fascinating, unforgettable day for Chelsea, a day of sunshine, laughter, entertainment and ... and *marvellous* company! Whether she had entertained Ricardo, she didn't know. But he had certainly entertained her in showing her the very *guts* of Madrid!

'Thank you for this day, Ricardo. It was wonderful!'

It was the third time she had said it and Ricardo looked at her pale, freckled face, a face framed with chestnut-coloured curls. He searched the clear, green, wide open eyes which for the moment held no worries, no fears, and he smiled. 'I'm so glad you enjoyed yourself, *niña*,' he said quietly. 'Because I certainly did.'

She looked up at him from her inferior height. There was something in his eyes she'd never noticed before, a light which she couldn't identify. How she wished she could! Had he really enjoyed himself or had he been bored? Was that a fleeting ... sadness ... she was detecting or was it merely weariness? It had been a long day ...

She didn't stop to think about what she was doing, Chelsea rarely stopped to do that. She merely did what she felt like doing, reaching up to link her arms around his neck in order to plant a kiss on his cheek. His eyebrows went up in surprise but there was no amusement on his face.

There followed an awkward moment for her, however. As she kissed him, as her arms closed around his neck her pert, firm young breasts pressed against the hardness of his chest and before she could pull away, Ricardo's hands were flat against her rib cage and it was he who was pushing her gently away from him.

Now, the look on his face was most definitely odd. He said something about changing for dinner and Chelsea quickly retreated towards the stairs, muttering something about taking a shower. Her cheeks were aflame as she ran to her room, hoping desperately that she hadn't embarrassed him by kissing him . . .

What could she wear to dinner? she was wondering a few minutes later, while, in another room, Ricardo Colchero was wondering why suddenly he was feeling so tense. He came to the conclusion that he had walked too far and talked too much for one day.

He ran a bath and stripped off his clothes, grinning broadly at the memory of the day, of Chelsea's questions. The girl asked so many questions! And when she listened, she listened avidly. When she gave her opinion, she gave it passionately. Ah, how young she was, young for her years, too. But she was so refreshing in her zest for, quest for, information and experience. Fleetingly he thought it a pity she wasn't a little older, that he couldn't show her how exciting Madrid could be at night.

Mercedes solved Chelsea's clothes problem. She got back to the house at eight, in time for dinner. In a mild state of excitement she tapped on Chelsea's door and they exchanged news briefly about their respective days.

Chelsea wasn't interested in the detailed description of what the young bride, a friend of Mercedes from her old school, had worn, but she listened until she could stand it no longer. 'Please! Don't tell me what colour her stockings were and what kind of shoes she had on! Your description of her head-dress took four minutes!'

Mercedes sighed in blatant exasperation, which was, for her, quite something. Normally she wouldn't be so rude to someone, she would have more control. But this girl, well, since they were going to go to the same school together, probably, they might as well learn to relate honestly to one another. 'Chelsea, you are *hopeless*!'

'Never mind that, tell me what you had to eat at this grand wedding. I mean, tell me something *interesting*!'

'Take that dress off. It doesn't suit you. I told you not to buy it! Those vertical stripes make you look even skinnier than you are. Isn't that obvious to you? It should be!'

Eyeing herself in the mirror, Chelsea thought she looked okay in the simple black and white dress. 'But I'm having a fat day today, so it's all right.'

'A fat . . .? What are you talking about?' The Spanish girl shook her head helplessly. 'It's awful. Take it off. I'll find you something of mine to wear. Again,' she added pointedly.

With a sudden fit of the giggles, Chelsea looked at her with a new respect. 'You know, I think you might be right. But you're being rather bossy tonight, aren't you?'

'I've decided it's the only way with you. You are too—too everything, Chelsea! You have no dress sense, you're too thin, too pale, too stubborn and too . . .' she would never have found the word, had she been speaking in English, so it was as well she was speaking her mother tongue, '. . . scatty,' she finished.

Open-mouthed, not knowing whether to protest or collapse with laughter, Chelsea said, 'Yeah? Is that all? Well, I like you, too!' Curiously enough, she was beginning to. She was beginning to like Mercedes as much as she liked her brother. She was even beginning to wish they were her own siblings, she'd always longed for a brother or a sister, or, preferably, both.

So when Mercedes issued her invitation the following morning, Chelsea was very tempted to accept. The girls were up early and were sitting near the fountain in the courtyard, alone, when Mercedes invited Chelsea to stay in Spain. 'Do you have to leave tomorrow? Our family has a house in Guadalajara. We often use it as a holiday home. In fact we have several houses in various parts of the country but the one in Guadalajara is my favourite. It belongs to Ricardo, actually, and it's in the hills, near a lake and—well, I wondered whether you'd like to come and stay with us? We're leaving on Tuesday to spend Easter there. Do say yes, Chelsea!'

Very touched, Chelsea considered it. She knew her father wouldn't mind; he wouldn't miss her company on the vacation he'd planned. In fact, he'd probably skip it and stay in New York and work. 'I—who's going, exactly?'

'My youngest uncle and aunt, who you met the other evening, and their son, who's three. Uncle Augusto, who's elderly and a widower. He's retired from the bank. Then there's me, my grandmother, Ricardo and his girlfriend Joelle, who's a lovely person. You'd like her. She's French, actually, but she lives in Madrid ... Why do you look surprised?'

'It must be a big house!' Chelsea laughed.

'It is.' The other girl seemed to take that for granted, just as she took it for granted she'd be surrounded by her family on her holiday.

'Will you let me think about it? I'm very grateful,' she added quickly, honestly, 'and I'd really love to come but ...' She was thinking about her resolution, about the talk with her father which she hadn't yet managed to have. 'I'll give you an answer by lunch time, okay? One more thing, have you asked Ricardo about this? Wouldn't he mind?'

'He approved,' Mercedes assured her. 'Naturally I asked him first. He thought it a nice idea.'

It was. But Hal Prescott vetoed it.

When Chelsea spoke to him in private about it, he said no. Ironically, it was he who wanted to talk to her. That's what he said, that he wanted to spend some time alone with her, to have a long talk with her.

Had she not been so surprised by this, Chelsea might have argued the point. As things were, it was inarguable. Hal was offering her the chance she'd been waiting for and she couldn't deny her pleasure on learning that her father did want her company, after all.

They left for the States the following day.

CHAPTER FOUR

'THIS bra's choking me, it's too tight.'

Mercedes made no comment. She was reading a letter from Ricardo, lying on the bed in the room she and Chelsea shared at the finishing school, L'Ecole du Vilier, which was some twenty kilometres north-west of Lucerne, Switzerland.

'What does this sweater look like without a bra? Mercedes? Will you look at me? Merc!'

There was a response this time, though Mercedes didn't look up from her letter. 'Don't call me that. How many times do I have to tell you?'

Chelsea turned her attention back to the mirror. It was the end of November and it seemed that she had been slowly but steadily gaining weight since the summer. Even in the two-and-a-half months she'd been at this wretched school, she could see differences in her figure. She wasn't altogether sure she approved of them, either. It didn't seem fair that quite suddenly she had started to change shape; she had thought she was too old for that to happen. Surely, at the age of eighteen years and six months, it would stop now? She didn't mind the fact that she was one-and-a-half inches taller than she'd been at the age of sixteen, but this weight gain was getting out of hand. Being a late developer was one thing—being fat was quite another.

She turned to Mercedes again, wanting her opinion. 'Can I get away with it or am I too ... you know, too heavy?'

Mercedes finally looked up, her pretty features distorted slightly by the frown she was wearing. 'Ricardo has finished with Joelle!' She flung the letter on to her bedside cabinet, her hands moving expressively as she made clear her disappointment. 'He's been seeing her for two years, and now, suddenly it's over.' She threw back her long black hair. 'Joelle has just gone back to live in France, he tells me, so that means the end of their relationship. Of course, he says that it isn't the end of their *friendship*, but still . . .'

'But still?' Chelsea was unaffected by the news, she couldn't see what Mercedes was fussing about. 'What?'

Her friend's soft brown eyes looked worried now. 'It's obviously the end of their romance, that's what.'

'So?'

'So? So I thought—hoped—he'd marry her, that's what!'

'Oh, Merc!' Chelsea flopped on to her own bed. 'Here you go again! Marriage is not the be all and end all in this life. There are other things, millions of them!' And Chelsea couldn't wait to get at them. But, for the moment, she was a prisoner . . . almost. She was ticking off each and every passing day, waiting for the Christmas holidays which she was going to spend in Madrid with Mercedes and her family. More importantly she was waiting for liberation day, as she thought of it. The day when she would leave this place, the day when she would be free. Free of routine, free of her dependence on her parents, free of the sense of obligation which both her mother and her father had managed to instil in her during the spring and summer holidays.

Oh yes, in their different ways they had managed once again to manipulate her. Her father had been immovable last Easter, and the time Chelsea had spent with her mother during the summer had been disastrous. They hadn't fought, not this time, not exactly. Maureen Prescott had been as adamant as Hal about her daughter attending the finishing school, so Chelsea had resigned herself to her fate. But there had been a heated exchange between her and her mother during which Chelsea had learned something, just one small piece of information which had never, ever, occurred to her before. It had come unintentionally from her mother's lips and . . . and she didn't want to think about it now, not now. It hurt too much.

She came back to the present and laughed at the way Mercedes was glaring at her. 'Don't let's get into that. We've agreed to differ on the subject, haven't we?'

On the subject of marriage and children and domesticity, they had agreed to differ. By now, they understood one another's points of view—and disagreed wholeheartedly. But, strangely, even this had contributed to the bond between them, to the friendship which had gone from strength to strength.

'It's just that I worry about Ricardo.' Mercedes picked up a second, unopened letter which had been in the post that morning, and Chelsea smiled inwardly as she saw her friend unconsciously hugging it to her breast. That letter had to be from her future fiancé. And she wouldn't open it now, Chelsea knew. Whenever there was a letter from Emilio, Mercedes would take herself off to the bathroom and lock herself in. She did this not only for privacy but also to escape any teasing she might be subjected to.

Poor Merc! In some respects she was so innocent. 'What are you talking about now?' she asked gently.

'When I marry,' Mercedes explained patiently. 'I'll be going to live with Emilio's family in Valencia.'

'May I remind you that you're not even engaged to the man yet? Anyhow, what's that got to do with your worrying about Ricardo?'

'Well, he'll be left on his own, of course!'

'What?'

'You heard me. I mean, who's going to run the house for him? Once I'm not there?'

With a click of her tongue, Chelsea asked the obvious question. 'Who runs the house now? Now you're not there?'

'My grandmother and the housekeeper.'

'So there you are!'

Mercedes would not be placated. 'Besides,' she went on, 'Ricardo's going to be thirty years old on the tenth of December.'

'What's that got to do with anything?'

'It's high time he was married, high time he started raising a family.' The words were out before Mercedes could think about them. The two girls looked at one another and started laughing. 'Sorry.' Mercedes shrugged as her laughter faded. 'I forgot myself there for a moment.'

They had ventured back on to their taboo subject and Chelsea was looking despairingly towards the ceiling. 'Okay, okay, so Ricardo's getting on in years, I'll grant you that. But maybe he doesn't want to get married, maybe he doesn't want kids.' Chelsea thought of Ricardo as her friend, her thoughts of him were nothing but kindly and, in her way, she was defending him now.

'You're being ridiculous. Ricardo loves children——'

'Right, so maybe he loves other people's children.'

'Oh, Chelsea! I meant—anyhow, what I was trying to say is that he'll need someone. And when my other brother finishes university ... both Ricardo and Vincente will need someone to look after them and run the house properly.'

Chelsea let out a low whistle. It was her way of warning Mercedes that her patience was running out. It was also something which upset and appalled the proprietress of L'Ecole du Vilier if she happened to be within earshot. *Madame* did *not* approve of 'her' young ladies whistling—for whatever reasons. To put it mildly, Madame du Vilier was a pain in the neck.

And Mercedes was still going on! 'Ricardo entertains a lot, you see, socially and for business reasons, what with the bank and his own property company, and all his contacts, and I'm wondering what will——'

'Wonder no more, dear girl.' Chelsea swung her legs

to the floor and shot a triumphant look at her. 'In that beautiful house of yours you have a staff of—how many?'

Mercedes looked puzzled but she answered quickly enough. 'Five, including the cook. Six if we include the chauffeur.'

'Oh, do let's count the chauffeur,' came the cheeky response. 'I mean, he also does his bit to look after a thirty-year-old man who's more than capable of looking after himself! Or is that something you haven't noticed about your brother? Ricardo can cope with anything, that's something I just happen to know about him, even if you don't.'

'Of course I know it. But that isn't what I meant, it isn't the same as——'

'Oh, for heaven's sake, Mercedes! Your housekeeper is competent, isn't she?'

'Very.'

'Right! Then shut up. Ricardo's got a competent housekeeper, so what does he need a wife for? Besides, they're surely one and the same thing. Except that not all wives are competent. So he's probably better off. He probably knows it, too, which is why he isn't breaking his heart over Joelle.'

'How can you know that?'

'I can't. I'm just guessing. She's only moved from Spain to France, and I can't see that stopping a man like Ricardo if he made up his mind to pursue her.'

Mercedes nodded slowly, thoughtful. 'You're right,' she sighed. 'I suppose it just wasn't meant to be.' She looked at her friend gratefully. When Chelsea wasn't letting off steam about something or other, she was often very logical in her thinking.

'Mercedes, darling, if you don't get off that bed, we're never going to get out of this dump! We're in parole time now. Let's get *out* of here!'

Parole time. It was Chelsea's way of reminding her that it was weekend, Saturday morning to be precise.

Heaven help the man who fell in love with Chelsea Prescott, she thought to herself. He would have his hands full. Would she ever settle down? Would she ever get rid of this—this discontent inside herself? A discontent Mercedes found difficult to understand.

She started dressing and noticed with amusement that Chelsea was changing her clothes for the third time that morning. It was flattering, the way she'd started asking her opinion about clothes, the way she was really trying to develop a dress sense of her own. Oh, but her lack of confidence in her physical attributes was pathetic. Beyond the bluster, the frequent outbursts, the apparent cockiness, Chelsea was a girl whose opinion of herself and her attributes and abilities was pitched extremely low.

The truth was that she was far prettier now than she had been when they first met seven months earlier. Her figure was filling out beautifully, the extra and much-needed weight had done wonders for her face, too. She looked healthy and vivacious with her light, bright green eyes and that hair of a most unusual shade. It was naturally curly, too. Mercedes almost envied her that. And Chelsea was clever, far cleverer than she herself, if she would only learn to accept that fact.

Against all the odds, Chelsea had turned out to be almost a model pupil—almost. From time to time she would do something outrageous, like whistling while she was cooking, like reverting into a slouching position while sitting at table or looking down at the floor while she walked, with her shoulders hunched.

It was during moments like that that Mercedes had come to realise fully that her friend was merely biding her time here at this school. Oh, she could turn her hand to anything if she chose to, and, since all conversation here was conducted in French, she was now speaking that language as well as she spoke Spanish. Yet she simply couldn't wait to be *free*, as she put it. Mercedes wasn't fooled; living with Chelsea she couldn't escape the feeling that one day there was going to be some sort of explosion. Though she frequently let off steam, whatever it was that ate at her regenerated itself and came bubbling to the surface over and over again. It was no use asking the girl what it was she wanted from life; she couldn't tell you. It wasn't that she wouldn't, it was that she couldn't. Not exactly. Clearly, she hadn't sorted it out for herself.

Still, for the moment things were under control and life was comparatively peaceful. But oh, how awful the first week here had been! Even Mercedes admitted that the school's rules and regulations, it's unreasonable curfew times, were more stringent than she had expected. According to rumour, no fewer than three girls from the previous year's class had got themselves pregnant during their time here, and Madame du Vilier had inflicted these new and unreasonable rules in an effort to see that this didn't happen again. She was frightened for the reputation of her school.

Chelsea had blown her top in the beginning. During the first week she had almost climbed the walls in her frustration. But not any more. She had, apparently, come quietly to accept that she was here until the following year and she might as well make the most of it. Not that she was even remotely interested in the opposite sex, Mercedes mused. That was another way in which Chelsea was seemingly slow to catch up with the rest of the world. Oh, she had a date today, true enough. If one could call it that. Both she and Mercedes were having lunch, and not for the first time, with a young German, the son of a man who owned a taverna in Lucerne. Klaus Schultz was someone Chelsea had got into conversation with, testing her German, she'd said, one Saturday when they'd gone in for lunch. The man was twenty-two years old and obviously fancied Chelsea like mad. But Chelsea had insisted that Mercedes go on these luncheon dates with her, that she wasn't interested in Klaus in a romantic sense.

'You know, Chelsea,' she said, thinking aloud now, 'there's something Madame doesn't seem to have taken into account when it comes to her girls' . . . protection.' She laughed at her own choice of word. 'I mean, since we're allowed out officially on Saturdays and Sundays, to go into town or do whatever we want, how come we're not chaperoned then? How come she trusts us?'

'She doesn't.' Chelsea pulled on her boots. 'But she thinks that night time is the dangerous time. The silly old bag must be under the impression that girls can't get pregnant during the day.'

'Chelsea!'

'Oh, shut up. She is a silly old bag!'

'Have you ever wondered what your old head teacher would say if she could see you now, if she could hear the way you talk? Take some of that lipstick off, it looks ridiculous. It's far too red for your colouring.'

Chelsea didn't argue about the lipstick. She wiped it all off. 'Mother Mary would be shocked out of her mind. But then Mother Mary was, is, merely one of life's innocents.'

'I see.' Mercedes suppressed a smile.

'What about this dress? Without the bra?'

'It's fine. You look nice.'

Chelsea's eyes moved from side to side as she examined her breasts. 'What about my boobs? I don't look too fat?'

'Oh, Chelsea! Won't you get it through your head that you're far from fat! You now have what I consider the ideal figure—enjoy it! Besides, breasts can't really look fat. They can look full but not fat.'

'Do mine look full? I mean, too full?'

Mercedes' face was wreathed in smiles. 'They look perfect—very sexy without your bra. I'm sure Klaus will enjoy looking at them!'

That proved to be quite the wrong thing to say. Their

escape was delayed for a further five minutes while Chelsea searched for a bra which wouldn't 'choke' her. She did not, she insisted, want to look sexy for Klaus. All she wanted from him, she insisted, was conversation in the language she was rapidly improving on.

On their way to the bus stop they stopped so that Chelsea could buy a German newspaper. She would pore over it, Mercedes knew, for at least an hour that evening, reading aloud, listening to her own accent. And then there would be the German records and cassettes.

The paper bought, Mercedes linked her arm through that of her friend as they walked briskly through the snow to the bus-stop. She was wondering what her own darling Emilio would make of Chelsea when they met at Christmas.

And what, she mused, would Ricardo make of her now? She had changed in many ways, some more subtle than others, in the seven months since he'd seen her. Would he approve of these changes? she wondered.

CHAPTER FIVE

'I HATE every minute of it!' Chelsea cried passionately. 'Ricardo, how can you possibly think I'm enjoying that school? I hate being obliged to do things, I hate being told what to do and I find most of the curriculum useless and pointless.'

Oh, it was so good to be back in Madrid! The city held something special for her, there was this lovely house, too . . . and there was Ricardo. Seeing him again had been like greeting an old friend. It was good to be talking to him, to be able to tell him how she was feeling. Ricardo really listened. He was so—neutral. He just listened and he made her think about things simply by asking questions. He never told her she ought— '*ought*' anything!

The rest of the household were in bed and this was the first long and private talk she'd had with him during the several days she'd been here. Tomorrow was Christmas Eve and more of the family would descend on the house. Ricardo's younger brother, Vincente, had already been here when she and Mercedes arrived. He had brought with him an English girl he'd met at Oxford, and Chelsea had liked both people on sight.

As far as Emilio was concerned, she was reserving her opinion. At first she had thought Mercedes' future husband too serious, almost dour. But she was keeping her thoughts and her comments to herself, bearing in mind how wrong her first impression of Ricardo had been.

'Useless and pointless?' Ricardo seemed surprised now. 'Yet Mercedes says you do everything so well. How come, if your heart isn't in it?'

She held up her hands, sighing. 'Because that's the

easiest thing to do. I mean, there's no point in fighting
the situation. I'm in it. I'm stuck there. I'm imprisoned.
All I can do is make the best of it.'

Ricardo nodded. 'That's a very mature way of
looking at it, handling it.' His eyes flicked over her as
she tucked her long legs under her on the sofa. She was
still often dramatic in her choice of words but she had
matured in some ways. She was self-conscious, though,
lacking confidence in herself and in her appearance.
That was something else his sister had told him, that
her friend wouldn't believe in her own attractiveness.
He hoped he'd be able to help a little in that respect.

'Mature?' she queried. 'I don't know about that . . .'

He surveyed her openly now. 'Mercedes has changed,
too. I think you're good for her, Chelsea. She's a little
more outgoing, less shy.'

'I don't know about my being good for Mercedes but
we are good friends. Maybe it's the attraction of
opposites!' She was pleased to think Ricardo was of the
opinion she was a good influence on his sister. Nobody
else seemed to think she was a good influence on
anything or anyone . . .

Her eyes rested pensively on the log fire burning in
the hearth as she tried to push intrusive thoughts of her
parents from her mind. Then she looked around the
room, snuggling herself more closely into the corner of
the sofa. She loved this room, the main salon. She loved
the entire house, she felt grateful to Ricardo for making
her feel this way in his home. It was on the tip of her
tongue to tell him, then, what she'd learned from her
mother last summer, to see what he would say. But she
held back. After all, her father was a business colleague,
so perhaps it wouldn't be right . . . 'Have you heard
from my father lately?'

'Not personally. His business with the bank concerns
my uncles more than me.'

'Mercedes tells me you own a property company, too,
you personally. That it's something quite separate from

your interest in the bank. I'm wondering how you manage to make so much time for your family? I mean, my father can hardly make time for——'

When her voice trailed off, he prompted her. 'For what?'

'For anything,' she said sullenly. 'Except work. And it's the same with *her*, my mother . . .'

'Go on.'

She lowered her eyes, finding that she was unable to go on. 'No, there's—there is no more to say. I—that's just how it is.' She shrugged, looking up, giving him an impish smile. 'Why don't you answer some of my questions, for a change? What kind of properties do you build? Offices?'

'No, holiday homes. Second homes of one kind or another. By that I mean they vary enormously.'

'But how many people want a holiday home in Madrid?'

'I don't build them in Madrid, *niña*,' he answered laughingly. 'I build mainly, though not wholly, in Andalusia. On the south coast, where the sun shines for the best part of the year.'

'Around Marbella, I'll bet?'

'Give or take a hundred kilometres either side.' He grinned as he saw her yawning. 'I can see that if I tell you much more about my business, you'll be asleep in no time! So tell me more about you, have you had any new thoughts on what you'll do with yourself eventually? On your career?'

'My career?'

'That is what you want, isn't it? A career?'

'Well, yes, I—or perhaps a business of my own. I—I haven't decided yet.' She looked away, yawning again.

Ricardo got to his feet at once. 'Right! It's bedtime. Come on, tomorrow's going to be a very full day.'

It certainly was! First thing the next morning, Chelsea went out to do some last minute shopping. Mercedes didn't go with her; not only had she bought

all her Christmas presents on their previous ex-
peditions, she also had time for little other than
Emilio. For all her organisation and domestic capa-
bilities, it was not Mercedes but Chelsea who checked
that everything was in order in the dining room at
noon, and Chelsea who arranged the fresh flowers for
the table. It was also Chelsea and not Mercedes who
soothed and helped the Colcheros' temperamental
cook when there was an accident in the kitchen
(caused by one of the maids) which resulted in the
spillage of the sauce which was to be served with the
main course.

When the rest of the family descended from twelve-
thirty onwards, the house started buzzing with chatter,
with excitement and a hint of chaos which Chelsea
found herself both enjoying and coping with. When one
of the children complained of feeling sick as a result of
his car journey halfway across the city, she distracted
the child by giving him a supposedly very important job
to do. For this she received grateful thanks from the
boy's mother, Antonia, who was eight months pregnant
and feeling it.

'You are a very good girl, Chelsea. My family are so
fond of you, you know. We regard you as one of us.'
These words came from Doña Teodora, at whose side
Chelsea was sitting in the main salon during the
afternoon. 'And you're so good with children.'

Good with children? Chelsea looked blankly at the
old lady whose buxom appearance belied her bouts of
ill-health. Always, Doña Teodora was dressed in black,
her posture perfect, her back ramrod straight, giving the
appearance of severity. But her eyes, so much like those
of Mercedes, were nearly always soft. And watchful.
When something was said or done of which she did not
approve, then and only then would her eyes narrow as
she let her displeasure be known. There had been times
when she had glared at Chelsea for committing the sin
of sitting with an ankle hooked over her knee, or

chewing gum or calling loudly to Mercedes from one room to another.

Generally in awe of her, liking her and unable to feel anything but respect, Chelsea always responded at once to Doña Teodora's methods of correction, just as she responded with great pleasure now to her compliments. The old lady had an air of power about her, as did her eldest grandson, and her great age gave her as much authority as Ricardo had, yet very often she would refer to him, with a look or a word, for approval on certain matters.

She did that now. 'Isn't that so, Ricardo?'

Her grandson turned from where he stood, glass in hand, near the fireplace. 'What were you saying, *Abuela*?' he asked softly, his black eyes gentle on her. He nodded, making no comment as his grandmother repeated the remarks she'd made to Chelsea. 'And isn't she looking smart today?' she went on as though Chelsea weren't there. 'I approve enormously.'

This time there was a comment forthcoming. Ricardo let his eyes move slowly over Chelsea from top to toe while he nodded slowly, approvingly. 'So you should,' he agreed, 'though smart is not the word I would have used.' His eyes flicked briefly to Chelsea's as he added, 'Attractive is the word I'd have used.'

She blushed furiously, relieved when Ricardo turned away again and grateful that the rest of those present were distracted in their own conversations.

On Christmas morning, Maureen Prescott telephoned to wish her daughter a Happy Christmas. Chelsea was locked in her bathroom when a maid came looking for her. *'Señorita, su madre esta al teléfono.'*

Chelsea stiffened, stepping into the bath and swishing the water noisily. 'I'm in the bath, I can't come. Tell her I send the season's greetings.' It was as much as she could do and be honest about it. Her father had phoned the previous evening and she had found it difficult enough talking to him. She had no wish to speak to her mother. On this day or any other. This was only a duty call in any case, as was everything else Maureen did for her daughter, little as it was. Duty, just duty.

Ricardo learned what had happened with Maureen's call, however, and he called Chelsea into the study to ask her about it later in the morning. It seemed that nothing escaped the head of the household. 'It is Christmas Day,' he reasoned. 'Don't you think it would be a nice gesture to return your mother's call and give her your good wishes in person? And your love.'

Her eyes widened, changing instantly to a lighter shade of green as her temper flared at his last sentence. 'Love? *Love?* I'm not a hypocrite!' she added hotly, bringing a frown to his face. 'I don't love my mother, any more than she loves me!'

'Chelsea! What are you saying? How can you think——'

'What? That she doesn't love me?' She spun away from him, heading for the door. 'It's just something I happen to know, that's all.'

To her surprise, he let it go at that. He let her leave the room without any attempt to stop her. In a way, she wished he had stopped her. Though she told herself over and over again that she didn't give a damn about what her mother had let slip, it kept coming back to gnaw at her.

The rest of the holidays was a huge success but it was New Year's Day—night—that proved to be the unforgettable part for Chelsea. She was supposed to be going out with Mercedes and Emilio that night to a dinner at the house of some of their friends. Ricardo was going elsewhere, to a party, and Vincente and his girl had already left Spain to spend New Year in England with her parents.

It was during the late afternoon that Ricardo came to Chelsea's room and asked her whether she'd rather go out with him. She was sitting in an armchair, reading, and was surprised when she heard a knock and opened the door to find him standing there.

'Come in.' Without a thought, a qualm, she invited him into her room, making no attempt to hide her pleasure as he settled in the other velvet-covered armchair.

'Unless you're particularly bothered about going out with Mercedes and Emilio tonight,' he said, getting straight to the point of this unprecedented visit to her bedroom, 'I'd regard it as a favour if you'd come with me to this party I'm invited to.'

She sat, confused by several different thoughts and questions racing round her mind. Her immediate reaction was one of pleasure; she'd be delighted to go with Ricardo. Mercedes and Emilio certainly didn't need her to make up a threesome! But why was Ricardo asking her? And what kind of party would it be? Did she have something appropriate to wear? Most importantly, would she be able to cope? Ricardo was a much older and very sophisticated man, she dreaded the thought of letting him down in some way.

'I—er.' She didn't get any further.

'You don't want to go with me? That's okay.' He shrugged, his voice and manner totally neutral.

Chelsea almost panicked. 'No! Wait! I mean yes. I mean I'd *love* to go.'

'You would?' He seemed amused and far from convinced.

'Yes! It's just—I—what kind of party is it?'

'Quite formal. No, don't look like that, all you'll need to do is wear something dressy and if you haven't got something suitable, Mercedes will have.'

Comforted by that, she asked her next question. 'What did you mean by saying you'd regard it as a favour if I'd go with you?'

'Well—shall we say there'll be someone present who'll try to monopolise my time, and if you're my escort it will make life easier for me.'

She was grinning broadly now and Ricardo followed suit. 'A woman! Ha!' She was highly amused. 'Why don't you just avoid the party altogether? She'll never believe for one minute that you're interested in *me*!'

Ricardo thought carefully before he answered that one. If he confirmed what she'd just said, it wouldn't do much for the confidence he was subtly trying to give her. 'I don't know what she'll think, nor do I care. I know only that when I leave the party, I'll be leaving with you. And I can't really avoid going, it's at the home of someone I do a lot of business with.'

It was settled. He left her, saying that they wouldn't be leaving the house till late, around ten o'clock. This left Chelsea hours in which to get ready. The idea of taking a nap was out of the question. She was too keyed up and worried, almost on the verge of changing her mind several times. A formal party with a business colleague. Herself as Ricardo's escort. It was going to be very different from the parties with the family.

'Are you *sure*? And what about shoes?' She was in Mercedes' room several hours later, having fetched the dress her friend said she should wear. Mercedes had picked it out for her on a shopping trip the previous week, along with several others, but it was one Chelsea had not yet worn. She took her friend's word about the dress, even though she absolutely did not feel right in it. It was a simple garment, made from a silky material, but in Chelsea's opinion the skirt clung too much and emphasised her too-rounded bottom. The bodice was demure enough and not cut too low, but it was sleeveless and Chelsea didn't like showing so much shoulder and bare arms because her skin was so pale. The colour wasn't right, either. Not for her. It was somewhere between Royal blue and navy.

However, when she put on the high-heeled, strappy shoes Mercedes was lending her, and wrapped a stole around her shoulders, she felt better. 'Okay, if you say so.' She took everything off and headed back to her own room. 'I've got to take a bath. I'll do my face and hair and then I'll come back for your inspection.'

'Chelsea, Emilio and I are leaving the house in five minutes. It's almost eight o'clock.'

'Oh, my God!'

Mercedes sauntered over to the door and gave her a quick hug, a reassuring smile. 'You don't need my inspection. You'll look right and you will behave splendidly, I just know it. Now don't worry. Enjoy yourself!'

Chelsea heard the clock in the hall strike ten but she couldn't bring herself to walk downstairs. She was as nervous as a cat and she looked *awful*. She had put make-up on and had taken it off again, reapplying just the tiniest bit of mascara on the tips of her lashes and some gloss which was the colour of her lips. She didn't look right with make-up, nor did she look right without it. And her hair—why hadn't she believed Mercedes when she'd said that the way to straighten her curly hair was to put big rollers in it? She could have bought some, she wished she had. Needless to say, Mercedes didn't have any rollers; oh, how she envied that girl her incredibly long, wavy mane of jet black! Her own hair was neither auburn nor brown, neither long nor short. Not these days. It just touched her shoulders and did its own thing.

She dropped her hairbrush at the sound of Ricardo's voice outside her door. 'Just coming,' she managed, smoothing her dress, looking at herself yet again in the full-length mirror. She was going to watch his face carefully when she opened the door to him—and if she saw any disappointment whatsoever, any disapproval, she was not going to the party. Definitely.

But she didn't see either of these things. When she opened the door to Ricardo her breath caught in her throat and for long, long seconds she forgot all about her own appearance.

The sight of him came as a shock to her. In black, immaculately cut trousers and a snow-white dinner jacket he seemed taller than ever, the *casta*, the pride bordering on arrogance, was more apparent than ever, compelling one's eyes to him, creating an intrigue about him. She stared at him, taking in everything about him, the darkness of his skin against the brilliantly white jacket and shirt, the features of a face she had never looked very closely at before, not as she was doing now. Even when she had been standing closer than the five feet she was standing from him now, she had never noticed how classic was his bone structure, the angle of his jaw, the firm, square chin. Nor had she noticed quite how his mouth was shaped, the curve of his lips, the Roman nose, the density of his brows above eyes as black as coals.

He was, she thought, not merely striking. He was handsome.

'You look beautiful, Chelsea.' Ricardo smiled gently and then chuckled as she blushed furiously. Flustered, disbelieving, she turned uncertainly to reach for her small evening bag, trying desperately to think of something to say in return.

Ricardo watched her as she moved awkwardly, self-consciously towards the dressing table. He saw her as he wished she could see herself, as a very young and very lovely girl. He looked over her figure as she put the stole around her creamy-white shoulders, allowing not the slightest expression to touch his face as he acknowledged privately what a delightful shape she was. Her dress was perfect for her, as was its colour, though the girl ... young woman ... was clearly not happy with the way she looked.

When he realised she was standing perfectly still, waiting, when he registered that he had been staring— and enjoying himself possibly too much in the process—he snapped out of it at once. 'You don't believe me? Since when have I told you any lies?' He held out an arm in invitation.

Chelsea slipped her hand through his arm, appeased but not convinced. She searched his eyes. 'My hair . . .?'

'Your hair.' Ricardo reached with his free arm to touch her hair as though it were something precious. 'Your hair is your crowning glory tonight, Chelsea.'

If she hadn't known better, she'd have thought he was flirting with her. Still, what he was doing was making her feel good. Maybe Mercedes had been right when she'd once said that her brother was kind. He was certainly understanding, he knew how nervous she was.

'You know, Ricardo,' she said laughingly as they strolled arm in arm down the sweeping, circular staircase, 'you're really not a bad old stick.'

'Why, how kind, *niña*!' He roared with laughter. 'But less of the "old", if you please. At thirty, I don't feel I fall into that category. Not quite.'

'And less of the "*niña*",' she countered. 'At nineteen, I don't feel I fall into that category. Not quite.'

'You're eighteen,' he said, shaking his head at her.

'But I'll be nineteen this year ... oh, yes I will!' She held up a hand, determined not to be contradicted. 'Today is the first of January, remember?'

Remember?

Remember. Ricardo Colchero was to remember the first of January more often than he could know at that point. He helped Chelsea into his car and slid in beside her. His driver knew where they were heading.

Only ten minutes later the car pulled up on the drive of an enormous house. Lights were spilling from every window, laughter and music was being carried on the cold night air.

Through seemingly endless introductions, questions, small-talk and some rather highbrow conversation, Chelsea sailed, and coped well as she and Ricardo circulated among what must have been more than a hundred guests. At one point they got separated, each in different groups of people, but her confidence never wavered, because he was in sight. And as long as he was there to give her a smile, an imperceptible nod which told her how pleased he was, she was all right.

Her confidence grew.

It was almost midnight before the food was carried into the vast salon and Chelsea had to stop herself from pouncing on it. As Ricardo took her arm and guided her towards it, she told him plainly, 'I'm starving. It's about time they fed us!'

He didn't say anything, he just tried unsuccessfully to suppress his laughter. '*Niña*, you make such a refreshing change, such a delightful escort!'

'Don't call me that, not here. I'm tired of having to explain to people who I am. A friend of Ricardo's sister. They all think it odd that you've brought me here, I know they do.'

'But there's one man who's grateful,' he informed her.

'Oh?'

Ricardo nodded across the room. 'Miguel Buendia— the man who keeps manoeuvring himself into your space. Or hadn't you noticed?'

'Are you kidding?' Chelsea stared openly at the man in question. 'Ricardo, he's got to be forty if he's a day!'

For the merest second the amusement left his eyes. 'He's three years older than I.' Then he was smiling again, concentrating on his food. 'What did you make of our host? Give me some more of that pâté, would you?'

'Not a lot. His wife's *beautiful* . . . speaking of which, have you seen *her* yet?'

'Who?'

'You know, the one who'll want you to take her home and make mad passionate love to her.'

'What? How much champagne have you had?'

'Two glasses.' She giggled.

'Three. And that,' he said, tapping the glass in her hand, 'is your last!'

'It was just a joke, Ricardo.' She looked up at him, unsure whether she had shocked him or irritated him or what.

'It was just another of those dramatic conclusions you jump to without sufficient information or thought.'

Her eyes widened. Quietly, a little shocked she said, 'Do I? Is that—is that something I do all the time?'

Something tugged at his heart as he looked at her then, at the clear green eyes so full of trust and innocence. He had been less than careful in his choice of words because she'd irritated him with her remark about the man across the room and the remark about the woman he wanted to avoid. He put down his plate and slipped an arm around her shoulders. 'Sometimes, *niña*. But no, not all the time. Hey, have they taught you how to dance properly at that lousy school you're going to in Switzerland?'

'They didn't need to.' She smiled, relieved that everything was all right again. 'Some things just come naturally to me.'

Ricardo led her to the room where people were dancing, wondering what the hell was the matter with him tonight. His head was too full of this young girl tonight, he was being unnecessarily sensitive in every respect. He was reading all sorts of things into all sorts of things. He didn't like what he had seen in Miguel Buendia's eyes when he'd been talking to her . . . and even now, as they danced, the other man's eyes were on her. Nor did he like himself for the thought that had flashed through his mind in response to her last sentence.

Unconsciously he held her a little closer as they moved to the music, finding her extremely easy to dance with. All traces of awkwardness vanished while she danced. As the music changed she, too, moved a little closer so she was pressing against him, and something approaching shock shot through his body.

'What is it?' Chelsea moved away slightly so she could see him better. 'Are you all right?'

Looking down into the innocent eyes, he couldn't help smiling in spite of his disturbance. 'Yes, little one,

I'm all right.' But he kept a point of holding her further from him from then on.

He made no protest when, on getting back to his home, Chelsea said she couldn't go to bed immediately. She said she was too—too high from the evening and all the fun of it. Ricardo not only understood this, he agreed with her. 'We'll have a cup of coffee. Just one. Instant. The staff are in bed.'

So was everyone else. Chelsea went off to make the coffee, leaving Ricardo to make sure everything was locked for the night.

He was in the main salon, a note in his hand, when she brought the coffee cups in. 'It seems your mother phoned again to wish you a Happy New Year.' He handed her the note but she waved it away, resenting the intrusion it represented.

'I'm not interested.' She flopped down next to him on the settee nearest the dying fire, keeping her head averted as she reached for her cup of coffee. But she never made it. Instead her hand was caught by Ricardo's and he shook it slightly, urging her to look at him.

'What is it, Chelsea? Why the tears in your eyes?'

She couldn't answer. She was too angry, suddenly, burningly angry.

'Come on,' he said softly. 'Why don't you tell me what this is all about? Your mother phoned on Christmas Day and then again this morning. And now tonight. Why won't you speak to her? What is it she's done that's so awful?'

That made her think, hard. What is it she's done that's so awful? 'It isn't what she's done—what she did—it's the way she's coped with it that's awful!'

Ricardo waited, wondering.

'I mean, she accuses *me* of being irresponsible. What a nerve!' Angrily she got to her feet, unable to sit still any longer. 'All my life, all my life they haven't given a damn about me! Do you know that? Neither Hal nor—

especially *her*. And do you know why? Because her career was more important, because she never wanted to get married in the first place. Yet she stays married to my father. Can you credit that? Can you understand it?'

That required an answer. Ricardo looked at her solemnly, at the defensive way her hands were stuck on her hips, at her readiness to attack not only him but everyone else in the world. 'You're not making sense, Chelsea. Why don't you tell me from the beginning?'

During the next half hour, through talking about it, Chelsea grew calmer and calmer, though she was no less upset. She was merely more controlled. She talked about her life, her childhood, how her parents had separated when she was seven because her mother couldn't stand living in New York. 'That's where my father's career was, with the bank, and that's where he wanted to stay. When he'd met my mother in England years earlier, she was a beautician and was in the throes of buying her own small business. She comes from an ordinary family and had no money to speak of. But she had ambition, as did my father. Lots of it.'

She was sitting again. She looked at the man by her side, suddenly realising he must know much of what she'd been telling him.

'Some of it, yes.' He smiled slightly. 'Now, why don't you tell me what's happened fairly recently to upset you so much?'

'It was last summer,' she said dully. 'You see, I've always *tried* to tell myself that my parents care very much, even when the evidence has been to the contrary. But last summer when I stayed with my mother, we talked about the finishing school thing and I told her I'd resigned myself to going but that there was no way I would go on to university afterwards. She got very angry at that. So did I. I couldn't understand why my continuing education mattered so much to her, when *I* couldn't care less about it. Eventually I yelled at her that I didn't know why she'd bothered to have a child in the first place if she'd never wanted to take any interest in it. I also went on to say I didn't know why she'd bothered to get married, either, since she obviously hadn't wanted to stay married. And her answer was . . . equally as loud and angrily, her answer was . . .'

Ricardo saw it coming but he said nothing. He wanted her to say it, to get it out. He watched as she dipped her head, avoiding his eyes in the mistaken belief that he would be shocked, or something.

'She said, "By God, I wish I hadn't, believe me! But I didn't exactly plan on having you, young woman! I never planned on marrying at all, but I was obliged to!" So that was that.'

Ricardo moaned softly, not fooled by the bravado with which she'd said the last four words. 'So it wasn't what she did that was so awful, I agree. She got pregnant and she didn't intend to, like thousands of other women. But you're wrong in saying she doesn't care about you and never has——'

Her head came up swiftly. 'That doesn't matter!' she shouted. 'I'm *not* wrong, but it doesn't matter. I've always known she has no time for me. I can accept that, I'm not a child any more. I don't need to try and fool myself any more. It's just that——' Her voice broke as tears spilled over and trickled down her cheeks. She finished on a whisper. 'It's just that . . . I wish . . . I wish she hadn't told me that . . . that she'd never wanted me in the first place.'

As she started crying in earnest, Ricardo gathered her into his arms and pulled an immaculate handkerchief from his top pocket. 'Here, *niña*. Sshh, now . . .' He held her as she alternately wept and blew her nose, thinking about his own parents, thinking about Hal and Maureen Prescott. At length Chelsea grew quiet but she made no attempt to draw away from him. Her head was resting against his shoulder as he held her and he spoke to her gently but positively, his lips almost brushing her hair. 'Believe me, Chelsea, your mother and father can't be anything but proud of you.'

She didn't believe that but she said nothing. She didn't want to move from the warm strength of his arms.

Ricardo was marshalling his thoughts, knowing he had to say something which would counteract the hurt she was feeling. He was glad she wasn't looking at him, because his own anger was considerable. It had been careless of Hal's wife to come out with that information the way she had. Hadn't she realised the damage she could do to a girl who was already convinced of her own worthlessness? She hadn't believed in herself before last summer. And now ... 'Chelsea, you must take my word for it that you are an important, intelligent individual who has many talents, not to mention good looks. Your parents cannot possibly be anything but proud of you, even if they didn't plan on having you. You're here, you're a clever and lovely girl and you're theirs. Despite your differences, which will resolve themselves in time, they do love you. I know they do, they must. How could they not?'

Chelsea listened to every word and believed none of it. She knew only that it was good to be held by him, that he meant well. Totally relaxed, she leaned against him, snuggling a little closer so that she became aware of the steady beat of his heart. In her entire life she had never cried as openly with anyone as she had in front of him tonight. But it was all right. And she was still listening to him as he spoke now of different peoples' ability to show their love, about how individuals differed when it came to demonstrating, being able to demonstrate, how much they cared for another person, about how the relationship between the people concerned was not always relevant.

He wasn't making much sense to her but that didn't

matter. Of course she realised he was referring constantly, though sometimes obliquely, to her parents' love for her. He was wrong, but that didn't matter, either. She knew only an overwhelming sense of gratitude towards him for the way he was trying to make her feel better. At one point, without thinking about it, she raised her head and brushed her lips against his cheek, returning quickly to the position she had been in lest he move away from her. But his arms were still around her; he didn't move at all and, really, she had known he wouldn't put her away from him this time, wouldn't be embarrassed this time. He cared about her, he cared enough to keep on talking, talking, and she adored him for it.

When she slipped a hand inside his open jacket, his speech faltered and she froze, dreading any kind of rejection when she so wanted, needed, the comfort of this physical contact with him.

At the sudden touch of her hand against his chest, Ricardo faltered in mid-sentence. Suspiciously his eyes moved to the top of her head; he could see nothing of her face. His own reaction to her touch disturbed him and he couldn't tell whether she was about to fall asleep on him or ... or whether she knew full well what she was doing. Gently he slipped his hand under her chin and raised her head so he might see what was in her eyes. They were moist and half-closed from sleepiness. 'Chelsea, I think it's time——'

She heard him, telling her it was time to go to bed, and for a few seconds she looked deeply into his eyes before her gaze shifted to his mouth. They were so close, it was easy to move the few inches so her lips could make contact with his. She helped herself to the briefest of kisses and was about to say good night when suddenly his hands slid to her upper arms and gripped her far more tightly than was necessary.

Her eyes widened in surprise, disappointment. 'Don't be cross, Ricardo!' she pleaded. 'Please! I only wanted to——'

'Cross?' He stared at her. 'I'm not cross. Chelsea, I——' He broke off, for once unsure what to say to her. 'Chelsea, you don't seem to——' He looked away, appalled at his longing to kiss her, really kiss her. It didn't make things any easier for him when his eyes came to rest on the soft swell of her breasts against the neckline of her dress. 'Go to bed, Chelsea!'

Her breath caught in her throat, her eyes narrowing in accusation as disappointment flooded her. 'See, you *are* angry with me!'

'No, no, I—oh, God!' She had looked at him with those half-closed eyes, the pink tip of her tongue flicking nervously over her lips. The next thing he knew, he was pulling her roughly against him, his mouth claiming hers with a force which made her go rigid in his arms. Instantly he eased up, forcing himself to kiss her gently—and briefly. He broke contact, his eyes searching hers almost fearfully in case he saw disillusionment in them.

He saw nothing in her eyes. She was just looking at him. Just—looking. 'Chelsea, one of these days you're going to realise——'

'What are you looking so concerned about?' She laughed at him. 'I have been kissed before, you know!'

Indeed? She sucked in her breath. Oh, he hadn't said the word. Sometimes this man could say so much with just the quirk of an eyebrow. It annoyed her now as it had annoyed her when she'd first met him, but this time she didn't show it. This time she kept her face expressionless, her voice soft, almost pleading. Two things were paramount in her mind: he didn't believe she'd been kissed before, which she had. She had therefore performed disappointingly, and that wouldn't do! Not for him. She also knew she wouldn't get near him again unless she was clever in using this . . . power . . . she was only just beginning to realise she possessed. 'Ricardo,' she whispered, 'you're hurting me.'

He let go of her at once and she looked down at the

red marks where his fingers had been biting into her arms. A trickle of shock ran down her spine, shock mingled with excitement as she realised he was more than she could cope with; she wouldn't bother experimenting further with him, after all! Instead she rubbed at her arms with both hands as Ricardo apologised.

'No, it was my fault,' she said honestly. 'I'm sorry, I don't blame you for being angry.' She got quickly to her feet.

'Chelsea!' Disturbed, he caught hold of her hand. She gave it a small squeeze as she stood, perfectly still, and for the second time that evening something tugged at his heart. He stood, still holding her hand, looking down at this girl-woman who had always interested him, often amused him. And tonight she was——

'Ricardo?' She was frowning. He looked as though he had a hundred things on his mind. It worried her. 'What is it?'

His breath came out quickly, as if he'd been holding it. 'I—it's nothing, Chelsea, nothing at all. I'm not angry with you, I don't want you to think that.'

'Then what can I do to make you kiss me again?' she asked. 'I mean, just a good night kiss.' That was all she meant. It was important to her to end this night on the right note, without any tension or misunderstandings between them.

Which was precisely what Ricardo felt. He was aware of the responsibility he had taken on, aware that his behaviour towards her mattered very much. He had been trying to inspire confidence and self-assurance in the girl; he wasn't about to quit now. There was more than one way of kissing her good night. 'Try asking me.'

She asked.

But it all went wrong, for him and for her. To begin with, his kiss was like one he might have given to his sister on saying good night, as had been his intention, but Chelsea murmured a protest as he raised his head.

She put her arms around him and it brought her body into contact with his as she spoke. 'I want to thank you for a lovely——'

With a self-deprecating groan, Ricardo gave in to his longing. He put his hands gently against the soft, flawless skin of her cheeks and lowered his head, kissing her lightly but in such a way that her lips were coaxed apart. She met him more than half way, which was what he'd hoped for and what he'd feared. She was so young but, tonight, so very irresistible!

Chelsea was both excited and fearful. Even as she returned the kiss, she shifted so that her body was no longer touching his. She didn't even consider what the contact might do to him, it was her own reaction she was afraid of. Her heart started thumping unbelievably hard, her legs felt weak and though the source of her pleasure was the gentle probing of his tongue, only just inside her mouth, moving lightly between her lips, every other part of her body seemed to be affected by it. She wanted to cling tightly to him again—and she wanted to run. She couldn't decide which she wanted most.

She was both disappointed and relieved when Ricardo made the decision for her. He stepped away from her, his hands lingering merely for seconds against her cheeks before he released her and was not touching her at all.

He counted to three before he spoke. He was angry with both of them but mainly with himself. *He* should know better. With something of an effort, he smiled. 'Say good night, *niña*. Go now.'

She didn't ask why he wasn't going to bed, she couldn't really think straight so she simply said good night and walked a little too quickly from the room.

Ricardo sat down heavily and muttered under his breath. What the hell was the matter with him? He was thirty years old and she was eighteen, *eighteen*! At that tender age, twelve years was a hell of a difference. She didn't know anything from anything, for all her intelligence. She was almost backward in some departments of life, compared with some of her peers. Was he so lacking in control that he couldn't resist the charms of an eighteen-year-old?

But that was the devil of it, she didn't even know she had such charms! Yet that in itself had been part of her appeal. 'Bloody hell!' He was muttering again, his fingers raking through the curls of his hair. He had a sudden mental picture of what that girl might be like in a few years' time, when she was a woman, all woman, and very well aware of it.

It was enough to make him shift uneasily as he sat.

But Chelsea was not a woman, not yet. This was the here and now and if he wasn't very careful she would end up having a crush on him. He mustn't let that happen. He had to be a friend to her and nothing more. She needed friends. Oh, she had Mercedes, but in a different way, she needed him, too.

He resolved there and then never to lay a finger on her again.

CHAPTER SIX

No sooner was Christmas over than Chelsea was looking forward to the Easter break. Ricardo himself had invited her to Guadalajara, to spend her break with him and Mercedes, Donã Teodora, Vincente if he came over from England, and, no doubt, several other members of the family. Delighted by the prospect, she also realised she was looking forward to it too much.

On her return to school she threw herself into her studies with a vengeance. She had the option of taking shorthand and typing lessons and, although she didn't envisage ever using these skills, she took them. They were less boring than the alternatives and at least they *might* come in useful, one day.

She thought often about Ricardo, realising she had a crush on him. It didn't worry her. From the age of eleven she had watched girls fall in and out of love; she was mature enough to know it would pass. She determined not only to keep herself busy but to set about gaining another sort of education. She was spending too much time dwelling on the way she had felt when Ricardo kissed her, of how it had been unlike anything she had experienced before, and she was determined to make some comparisons.

So, every weekend during the term, she and Mercedes, with or without some of the other girls, went into town and had fun. Mercedes went solely for company, she would not accept even a luncheon date with someone of the opposite sex. She 'belonged', she said, to Emilio, and she didn't want anyone else, or even to discover whether she might want anyone else.

Chelsea's thinking was very different. She was deliberately making the effort to mix with as many

males as possible, which she discovered to her delight and
surprise was a very easy thing to accomplish. She was
beginning to realise that she really was attractive, though
her reasons for wanting to spend as much time as possible
in male company were not all for the benefit of her ego.
She was having difficulty in getting over her feelings for
Ricardo, more difficulty than she'd anticipated.

On the night before they were to fly to Spain for
Easter she lay awake in her bed, too excited to sleep.
She was longing to see Madrid and the house, where
they would spend their first night, and the people whom
she'd missed as though they were her own family. At
least, that's what it felt like; she couldn't really know
because she had never had a family life of her own.

On imagining what it would be like seeing Ricardo
again tomorrow, a portion of her mind protested that
she shouldn't go to Spain at all, that she was still too
emotionally vulnerable where he was concerned, despite
her efforts to find distractions.

But wild horses wouldn't keep her away.

The weeks of the Easter holidays, however, brought
disillusionment. Doña Teodora was not well enough to
make the journey to Guadalajara and Ricardo would
not leave her in Madrid, even with one of his relatives,
for more than a few days. He spent less than a week in
Guadalajara.

That short time was precious to Chelsea. Ricardo's
attitude towards her, his friendliness and attentiveness,
was just the same as ever. But not once did he look at
her in the way she wanted him to, as though she were a
woman. Oh, his compliments came readily but she
could sense his underlying detachment. He made no
attempt to be alone with her, nor did he try to avoid
being alone with her. In short, he made it clear that he
was a friend to her, nothing else. He did this very
effectively on the day she and Mercedes were leaving
for their last term in Switzerland, when he summoned
her to his study in the house in Madrid.

'Tell him I'll be along in a moment.' Chelsea leaned against the door of her room, listening as the maid acknowledged what she'd said and padded off down the hall.

The full-length mirror on the back of the door reflected a girl who was dressed for travelling. She sighed, pushed her hair back with her fingertips and made her way downstairs. As she walked to Ricardo's study she moved slowly, taking a long and careful look at this lovely house, at the familar surroundings which had always pleased her so much.

Her heels clicked as she crossed the pink and grey marble hallway, letting her fingers trail over the Italian statues as she passed them, one by one. She had the saddening thought that she might never see this house again. That after today, she might never see Ricardo again. She paused by his door, trying to compose herself before going in.

'Good morning, *niña*.'

She forced herself to smile as she sat, facing him, but his greeting irked her far more than it ever had in the past. 'Good morning, Ricardo. I—mustn't stay long, I haven't finished packing,' she lied. She didn't want to be here, alone with him in his private room, so close but so separate. She wanted to flee.

'I missed you at breakfast.' He was smiling, watching her in that careful way of his.

'I—Mercedes and I were up long before you.'

He glanced at his watch, laughing a little. 'So—this is it, mm? Your last term of school and then—what, Chelsea? Have you reached a decision as to your future?'

'Who knows?' She shrugged. 'You know I intend to travel but what I mean is, who knows when it comes to the future?'

Ricardo surveyed her carefully. She was still changing. It amazed him always how she changed subtly from season to season. Looking at her now and thinking of the girl who had sat in this room with fear in her eyes only a year ago, the difference was so clear to see. A year. Just twelve months.

Nevertheless, she worried him now as she had worried him then. There were a few things he had to say to her now, while he had the chance. It was important. 'I'll go along with that up to a point, but we do have choices in life. Do you remember when I once told you to be careful about what you want, because it's what you'll surely get?'

She remembered very well. 'I didn't understand you at the time. Or maybe I didn't believe you. But I do now. I think you should qualify the statement, though, I think you have to want something very, very much to be sure of getting it.'

He smiled without humour. 'Absolutely. You have to want with a passion, until you are living and breathing it, and you have to have faith.'

In whom? she wondered. But she didn't ask. All she wanted to do right now was to cry. Again she shrugged. 'Well, there's nothing I want with such fervour, nothing in life I feel so strongly about. All I want is my freedom and some fun, it's all I've ever wanted.'

Ricardo looked down at his desk. He didn't know how to caution her further without sounding like an uncle, which was something he'd always avoided. 'My cousin Juan says you told him you wanted to have a "good time". I think your choice of words worried him.'

Ricardo was grinning but Chelsea was not amused. 'Do all the family report in to you? Last night you told me how nice it was I'd spent so much time with Antonia's children in Guadalajara—after you'd left.'

'Hey, why so aggressive?' Her tone surprised him. 'Surely you don't resent the fact that we all care about you, take an interest in what you do?'

She looked away. No, it gave her more joy than he

could know that her family—Mercedes' family—were so warm and loving.

'And we all worry about you to different extents. Juan a little more than others, perhaps.'

Her eyes moved swiftly back to his. 'What do you mean by that?' The aggression had gone, she asked this with real curiosity.

Ricardo chuckled. 'I think you know very well, madam, that my young cousin ... admires you.' He knew all about her flirtations in Switzerland, too, though he realised he'd better not mention this. Poor Mercedes, she worried about this girl more than the rest of them put together! His amusement disappeared. 'Chelsea, if ever you're looking for a job, you have one with me. I want you to know that. If you decide you want to start work come summer, come to me. If, on the other hand, you're still determined to take off on your travels, just—just be careful. I mean, be careful generally. In your eagerness to live, as you put it, and in your thirst for new experiences, don't grab too eagerly. Have respect for yourself, and others will respect you. Remember that you're an important and worthwile individual, then others will remember it, too. Don't plunge headlong, without thought, into something—anything—which might adversely affect you and your future, or your peace of mind.'

Chelsea stared at him, delighted and bemused. A job? He was offering her a job? She had no idea what use she would be to the Colchero bank but the offer was sincere, she knew, and she was more than gratified. As to his warning—what was it he was warning her of, exactly? Anything and everything? She didn't know how to answer him. 'Th-thank you. I mean, about the job——'

'And there's no time limit on the offer. Remember that, too, please.' He stood up. 'In the meantime, good luck, niña.'

'Aren't you driving to the airport with us?'

'I'm afraid I can't. I have a luncheon date with Maria.'

Maria, the woman he'd been out with so late last night. His latest mistress! Chelsea got miserably to her feet and bade him goodbye.

It was not until the following October that Mercedes got her first postcard from Chelsea. It came from Dijon in France. After that, in November, there came one from Luxembourg, and after that there was a brief letter from Brussels. Then in January of the following year there came a two-page letter from Rotterdam— which contained the promise of a longer letter soon.

The long letter arrived in April, with apologies for its delay, and it so shocked Mercedes that she went instantly in search of Ricardo. 'Cristina, *donde esta mi hermano*?' Appalled by what she had read, Mercedes asked the maid where her brother was.

'I'm here.' Vincente appeared in the doorway of the small salon, looking extremely pleased with himself. He had looked like that ever since he'd got engaged to Señorita Anna Hervas, whom he'd met last year, after he'd finished university and come home permanently.

'Not you, Vincente.' Mercedes was on her feet. 'I mean Ricardo. I must speak to him. Now.'

'I think he's just leaving . . .'

He was. Ricardo was in the hall, picking up his briefcase from a table when Mercedes caught up with him, still clutching the letter. 'Ricardo, I must talk to you!'

'But of course.' He didn't need to ask whether something was wrong. His sister clearly had something important on her mind, something that was upsetting her. He followed her into the salon and they sat, Ricardo listening carefully as she read out Chelsea's letter to him. All of it.

'What do you think of *that*?' she demanded when she'd finished. 'I mean, Chelsea working on a Kibbutz!

Can you imagine it? Whatever possessed her to do it? She's not cut out for that type of life, that type of work!'

Ricardo's answer came quietly and calmly, belying the frown on his face. 'Who can say what Chelsea is cut out for? Even she can't, or couldn't, tell us that. Maybe that's why she's doing what she's doing—she's finding herself.'

'But, Ricardo, she's spending her days picking fruit or peeling potatoes or cleaning out chicken sheds! How can that help her find herself, as you put it?'

Ricardo smiled, partly in sympathy for his sister, who would probably never understand. 'This,' he said, waving a hand towards the letter, 'and all the rest of the travelling she's done so far, is something she has to get out of her system. She'll survive, don't worry about her.'

'But I *do!*' Her eyes narrowed and she looked long and hard at her brother. It had never, ever, occurred to her before but . . . 'Ricardo, did you encourage Chelsea to do this?'

'What?'

'All of it! I mean, this is almost exactly what you did——'

'Certainly not.' At her dubious look, he added firmly. 'No, Mercedes, I never even mentioned to her that I'd done something similar when I was younger. I very carefully never mentioned that.' He took the letter from her and glanced over it himself. 'Well, at least you have a long-term address you can write back to now. And when you do, give her my regards.' He had noticed that Chelsea had remembered him in her postscript, her after-thought: 'Give my regards to Ricardo.'

CHAPTER SEVEN

SEVERAL months later Chelsea found a quiet spot where she could settle down to read Mercedes' latest letter. The letters came regularly, twice monthly, and they *always* began with, 'When are you coming home?'

'Home' meaning Madrid. Chelsea never failed to be pleased by Mercedes urging her to go and stay for a few months. It was nice to be welcomed by all the Colcheros, which she knew without doubt she was. And Mercedes loved her dearly, regarded Chelsea as the sister she had never had. She'd said as much. How odd it was that they were so close when they were so very, very different! How odd they had forged such a firm friendship during their year at school, when they had fought more times than Chelsea could remember!

Even now, when they had both turned twenty, after so many months and the exchange of so many letters, Mercedes was still obviously bewildered, if not appalled, by her friend's behaviour! In every letter Mercedes called her *loca*, crazy. Chelsea had tried to explain; more than once she had told Merc that the hard work here on the Kibbutz had a cathartic effect. The hard, physical tasks involved in working in various ways on the land had somehow served to help her get rid of her anger, her frustrations. She had become much calmer than she'd ever been, had learned to be more philosophical about life. Also she had admired and enjoyed the characters, the team spirit of her co-workers, the majority of whom were Jewish but by no means Israeli. She had met people from all corners of the world on the Kibbutz and, making her realise how small the world is, another New Yorker, David Lazarus, had been one of them.

Chelsea had had a platonic friendship with David, who was very much an intellectual. He had spent three months here and had moved on two weeks ago and, now, she was missing him so much that she wondered whether she'd been a little in love with him. She sighed on thinking about him, squinting against the brilliant, early October sunshine as she sat on the ground, her back resting against the building in which she shared accommodation with three other girls.

The blue airmail envelope from Mercedes was as yet unopened, it stayed that way for some time. Chelsea was deep in thought, her eyes focusing on the distant landscape, but no longer seeing. She had been to many places on her travels before reaching Israel, and it was dawning on her slowly that it was in fact not places which made her happy, it was people. She went on to think about her friends, those who had come and gone in her life and those who remained, like Mercedes. When the two of them had said goodbye at the end of the final school term, Mercedes had extracted two promises from Chelsea, the first being that she would write regularly, the second that she would not miss Mercedes' wedding.

Mercedes' wedding! It was still another year, almost, before she could marry Emilio, before he finished university, but the date had already been fixed. Oh, yes, Mercedes had written with *that* piece of information about three letters ago! She was to be a September bride. Well, Chelsea certainly had plenty of notice! She had replied and reiterated her promise: she would be at her friend's wedding come hell or high water! And so she would; how could she possibly miss the most important event in Mercedes' life?

Precisely five months later, to the day, Chelsea was sitting in the same spot, a new, unopened letter from Mercedes in her hand. But on this occasion she did not delay in reading it, she was anxious for news. She was feeling incredibly blue. Christmas had come and gone, and during that time her discontent with life on the Kibbutz had begun. It was March now and she was feeling an inexplicable need for contact with people from her past, though she had not the faintest idea why this should be so.

Two weeks later she was on a plane, heading for home. Not for Madrid but for England. Madrid would come later. She was going to stay with her mother for a while, for as long as it would—well, for as long as it would work. She was in fact almost eager to talk to her mother now. She looked down at her hands, grimacing. Her mother, a beautician and a stickler for grooming, would have a fit when she saw those hands. After so many months on the Kibbutz they were not exactly in good condition. In fact she was something of a wreck, she was physically tip-top as far as health was concerned but her skin was dry, her hair and her hands were coarse and her entire wardrobe consisted of battered jeans, shorts and T-shirts. She closed her eyes, hoping for—she wasn't sure what. Maybe, if things went well, she and her mother could spend a week in London, do some shopping . . .

Her thoughts switched to her father. She would go to New York to visit him, too. Perhaps . . . maybe there was a chance he could be persuaded to get on a plane and spend Easter in Torquay? It wouldn't be the first holiday he'd spent with his estranged wife, not by any means. If not, then she would go to New York to stay with him for a while.

After that, she would head for Spain. It was geographically the wrong way of planning these visits, but that was the order she wanted them to be in. Quite when she would get to Madrid, she couldn't say at this point. She knew only that she would be in plenty of time for Mercedes' long-awaited wedding!

A brief smile, a wry smile, flitted across her lips. Her own views on marriage had not changed, though in many other ways she had changed drastically. She was far more mellow, and she had finally decided what she would do with her life. In two months' time she would be twenty-one and from that day on she would be in control of a fair amount of money, which her father had put in trust for her years ago. She would go into business, in or around London, probably. A business of her own was surely the right thing for her. With such ambitious, successful parents, how could she fail? She simply had to be business-orientated. In fact she should have realised years ago that that was what she was cut out for.

The smile returned to her lips as some words sprang into her mind, Ricardo's words: 'Be careful about what you want . . .' Well, at least she knew what she wanted now, at long last.

She closed her eyes, thinking about Ricardo and the crush she had had on him at eighteen. Her smile broadened. It hadn't lasted long. And thank God he hadn't known about it at the time, she'd have felt such a young idiot! Her smile became a soft chuckle. Maybe she'd tell him about it when she saw him, it would be good for a laugh!

She thought also of many other things Ricardo had said to her, about her mother, about relationships. She remembered his words very clearly, oddly enough, though at the time she had thought they were going in one ear and out of the other. But no, she hadn't forgotten what he'd said to her, it was as if it had all been stored away, somehow, in her mind—until such time as she was ready to appreciate it.

It was with respect that she thought of him now, and with fondness, before she drifted off to sleep, wondering how he would appear to her these days, when she eventually got to Madrid . . .

CHAPTER EIGHT

RICARDO COLCHERO stood alone at the barrier near the exit from customs in Barajas airport in Madrid. It was eleven in the evening on the first of August. He was aware of a sense of anticipation which made him smile slightly. Where was she? Surely all the passengers on this flight had walked past him by now?

He glanced at his watch and turned to look behind him. Maybe he'd missed her, failed to spot her? No, he wasn't likely to do that. Perhaps there was a hitch with her luggage? He turned back to the barrier as the last few passengers emerged. Then, suddenly, there she was.

Chelsea was several yards away from him, her eyes glancing round swiftly for a familiar face. She was expecting to be met by Mercedes, not by him.

Ricardo didn't call her name, for seconds he couldn't have spoken if he'd wanted to. He watched her in those few moments with fascination and a pride he knew he wasn't entitled to be feeling. He was plunged back in time to the night when this girl, then an awkward and pugnacious, scruffy seventeen-year-old, had walked round this same barrier with her father.

And look at her now! In high-heeled, black leather court shoes she stood very tall and proud; poised, confident. He could see nothing of her hair beneath the black Cordoban hat she wore at an intriguing angle but he could see every curve and plane of her sumptuous figure, a figure shown to its best advantage in a close-fitting, white linen dress. He raised his arm in greeting, smiling as she spotted him and wondering whether he was about to meet a stranger.

Chelsea was momentarily rooted to the spot. Dear Lord, she had forgotten how very striking Ricardo was!

An overwhelming sense of pleasure engulfed her because she was here, at last, in the city she had fallen in love with a long time ago. She had so longed to see Madrid again, had looked forward so very much to seeing the Colchero family. All of them. Ricardo no more and no less than the others.

With her head held high she moved gracefully towards him, a fine example of all the poise and control which had been drummed into the girls by Madame du Vilier and her staff at the Swiss finishing school. 'Hello, Ricardo.' She smiled, offering her hand.

'Chelsea,' he said simply. He took her hand, content to greet her in the English tradition, with a firm but brief handshake. 'Mercedes sends her profuse apologies and begs to be forgiven that she isn't here to meet you. My grandmother is unwell and Mercedes was up with her all night last night, and today she's had a hectic time organising things. She'll see you in the morning.'

Chelsea nodded, frowning at the news of Doña Teodora's being unwell. She could imagine the froth Mercedes was working herself into, what with her grandmother being ill and her wedding being only a month away. 'I'm only sorry I couldn't get a flight that would get me in at a decent hour. I—what's wrong with Teodora, Ricardo?'

He shrugged, his black eyes momentarily losing some of their light. 'She's had an attack of bronchitis but—well, she's eighty-nine years old, you know. She's looking forward to seeing you, I'm sure you'll cheer her up.' He picked up her cases. 'Come on, my car's right outside.'

They walked to the doors, talking all the time, Chelsea being eager to catch up on news of all the family. Vincente had married Anna Hervas and was living in Barcelona, working at a branch of the Colchero bank. She had known that much but she was curious to hear whether he was enjoying married life.

'Very much so.' Ricardo glanced at her as they

passed through the doors. 'You can ask him yourself next month. He tells me there's much to recommend it.' He cocked an eyebrow, his eyes showing curiosity now. 'Why? Are you thinking of entering that fine old institution, Chelsea?'

'No way!' She laughed, her brows lifting as Ricardo opened the boot of a smart, ultra-modern sports car, a dark red Aston Martin Lagonda which must have cost every penny of the price of a Rolls Royce. 'Congratulations are in order for you, too. Mercedes wrote and told me about your book. It's coming out next month, isn't it? And by the way, this car is gorgeous! Congratulations again!'

He opened the passenger door for her, his eyes flicking over her long legs as she got in. 'I can assure you my book has nothing to do with the purchase of this.' He smiled, tapping the roof of the car. 'Just in case you were wondering.'

Chelsea smiled in return. She had not for a moment thought his book was going to add to his wealth. It was, according to Merc, a technical work on economics and banking. Hardly best-seller material! 'I look forward to reading it,' she lied, a twinkle in her eye.

'Of course you do,' he said drily. 'I'm sure you can't wait.'

Despite the teasing, now they were in the confines of his car she felt a slight tension between them. From the moment of his shaking hands with her so formally, she had not felt she was simply meeting an old friend. She'd been aware of ... something missing, perhaps. It was understandable, though. A great deal had happened to her in the past two years, and no doubt to him, too. For all they knew, they were strangers to one another now.

She looked at him surreptitiously as he drove away from the airport, master of this powerful car and of everything he touched or did, as ever. He was dressed casually in black, black slacks and a black cotton shirt which was open half way down his chest. He was a little broader, wasn't he, than he had been two years ago? Her eyes slid over the length of his body, from the obvious strength in his thighs to the magnificent chest which was covered with hair as black as jet. Her gaze lifted to the strong lines of his face, his incredibly curly hair. Gypsy! The same word sprang to mind, after all this time, and she looked quickly away lest he become aware of her scrutiny.

The staff hadn't changed, neither had the house. It enfolded Chelsea in its warm and welcoming vibes the moment she stepped into the pink and grey marble hall. Her eyes moved hungrily over the Italian statues, a table here, a clock there, and she turned enthusiastically to Ricardo—to find he was watching her intently. 'It's . . . I . . .'

His eyes held hers and he nodded. 'I'll take your case upstairs, Chelsea. You know your way to the salon. Cristina's on duty this evening, ring her and tell her what you'd like to eat.'

She was grateful for the coolness of the house. The heat that had met her as she stepped off the plane had been astonishing considering the hour. But then she hadn't actually been in Madrid in the summer before, hadn't realised how hot it could be.

'Have you sent for the maid?' Ricardo was back, pausing by the huge fireplace beside which hung the bell-rope that would summon the staff.

'Not yet. I don't want anything to eat, thanks, but I could certainly use a drink.'

'Tea? Coffee? Wine?'

'A gin and tonic with lots of ice.' She sank back into the comfort of the settee, kicked off her shoes and tucked her legs under her.

Ricardo smiled inwardly, pleased that she was making herself comfortable like this. He watched in fascination as she took off her hat and pulled two pins from her hair. Her hair was much longer than it had been, it tumbled around her shoulders in all its chestnut-coloured glory, thick, shining, looking quite wild now as she released it fully by running her fingers through it.

'Ah, Cristina . . .' He turned away, forgetting for a moment what he wanted of the maid. When she fetched the drinks, he dismissed her for the night. He would wait on Chelsea himself if there were anything she wanted.

'So,' he said at length, raising his glass to her. 'Here's to you, Chelsea Prescott.' He was sitting on the settee facing hers, his long legs stretched out in front of him. 'I understand you've been staying with your mother for the past few months? How did it go?'

'Unbelievably well.' Chelsea's face was sombre. It seemed incredible she'd had to wait until she was twenty-one years old before getting to know her mother. 'And I have you to thank for that.'

'Me?'

'Oh, yes, yes indeed. You know, I never forgot all the things you said to me, that night, here . . .' She gestured around the room, to the very settee she was now sitting on.

'The night of the first of January.' Ricardo nodded, remembering. 'All I did was to point out your mother's side of things. You might never have come to see things from her viewpoint, but you did, so all the credit is yours, Chelsea.'

'Perhaps. In any case, you were right in saying Maureen loves me as much as she's able to. And what more could I ask of her than her loving me as much as she can? She isn't the demonstrative type but I realise she cares very much about me.'

Her father had come over to England at very short notice last Easter and it had been very much a reunion, a family affair. There had been no tears, no recriminations, no airing of regrets or apologies or anything of that sort. None of them were sentimental people but there had been between them . . .

understanding. Yes, that was it. They each respected the other's independence and freedom to do their own thing. Easter had been a success.

Afterwards, there being no need to go to New York, Chelsea had stayed in with her mother. They had gone on a shopping spree in London and it was during that particular week that they had got to know each other quite thoroughly.

'I've lost you, Chelsea. Where have you gone?' Ricardo's voice cut into her thoughts and she looked up to find him watching her in that familiar, careful way of his.

'Sorry. I was still thinking about my mother. I worked in the office for her while I was there, thinking I'd stay as long as she wanted me around. I never dreamed it would last several months!'

'And what happened then? Did she kick you out?'

'No!' Chelsea laughed at him. 'Mercedes' wedding was on the horizon, that's what happened! I had a promise to keep. Though to be honest, I was beginning to get bored. I'm not cut out for life in an office.'

'What about life on the land? Were you cut out for that?'

'Temporarily, yes. Life on the Kibbutz was good.'

'Tell me about it.'

'Well, put it this way, if I never see another avocado, another olive, as long as I live, I'll never forget what they look like.' Her apple-green eyes were lit with amusement, followed by thoughtfulness. 'What can I tell you, really? I've seen the Wailing Wall in Jerusalem, I've strolled along the shores of the Dead Sea. I've met hundreds of people, I've fallen in and out of love two or three times—I think.' The twinkle was back in her eye. 'What can I tell you that you don't already know? Didn't Mercedes show you my letters and cards?'

'Some, but not all. You can imagine how that intrigued me!' His smile was roguish, his black eyes glittering devilishly. 'How come I didn't get to see all of them? What did you do that only your closest girlfriend may know about?'

Nothing, was the answer to that! Of course, she wasn't going to tell him so. Instead she tossed back her hair, laughing, wagging a finger at him. 'I think I'm entitled to some secrets nowadays, don't you? A little mystery?'

Ricardo inclined his head. 'If you say so.' Her long, slender hand covered her mouth as she started yawning. Everything she did, even the smallest things seemed to be graceful, utterly feminine . . . How she had changed!

He was aware she was tired but he didn't want to call it a night, not just yet. The next few weeks were going to be busy for everyone and he might not have the opportunity of talking to her alone for some time. He got up and refilled their glasses. 'Come on,' he coaxed, 'tell me all. What was the worst thing you did while on your travels, let's start with that.'

Chelsea didn't have to think about that. 'I drove without "L" plates before I got my driving licence—a battered old van which belonged to some Australians I hitched up with for a while. And I tried smoking pot.'

'And?'

She shrugged. 'Happily I didn't get hauled before a magistrate or involved in an accident. As for the pot—it made me vomit. I never tried it again.'

There was silence then. Chelsea found herself regarding him as he was regarding her. She was vaguely irritated, wondering what he expected of her, what he really wanted to know. She didn't have to wonder for long.

'So what conclusions have you reached?' he asked at length. 'About yourself, about life?'

Chelsea took a long swallow of her drink and glanced at her watch. 'It's a bit late to embark on that kind of conversation. If you're asking whether I know what I want now, the answer is yes. I'm thinking of going into business when I get back to England, in the London area. I've yet to decide what kind of business——' She broke off, laughing. 'I've yet to find a place to live, come to think of it! All the possessions I have in the world are in those two suitcases upstairs!' She finished her drink and got to her feet.

One dark eyebrow rose in curiosity. 'You're not exactly forthcoming, Chelsea.'

She shrugged. 'I don't mean to be abrupt, it's just that I'm shattered.' The gin, the hot weather and the journey were taking their toll.

Ricardo walked slowly towards her and put one hand on either side of her shoulders. He smiled and kissed her European-style, his lips brushing against both her cheeks. 'Welcome back.'

She looked directly at him, oddly disturbed by the belated greeting, by his nearness. She stepped away from him, disturbed even more by the touch of his hands. What the devil was the matter with her? She'd got over her youthful crush on this man years ago! Gorgeous to look at though he was, he wasn't even her type, basically! She'd realised that a long time ago, too.

'I won't keep you up any longer,' he was saying, 'except to say you're looking . . . looking very well.'

Was that all? She felt amused, challenged by his banal remark. In bare feet she was several inches shorter than he and she looked up at him again, an audacious smile coming to her lips as she tossed back her hair almost defiantly. 'Is that all, Ricardo? Is it really?' And then she laughed at him.

His own laughter was low and rumbling. He wasn't about to lie, nor would he deny a beautiful woman that which was her birthright. 'You know damn well it isn't.' One hand snaked out and caught hold of her chin. *Casta!* She had that, too. She had it and she wore it about her like a garment. 'You're beautiful, and you know it. You're revelling in it!'

He let go of her chin as roughly as he had taken hold of it, his eyes still on her as she bent to pick up her shoes and handbag. She walked away from him, laughing softly, turning just once to let him see the amusement in her eyes.

And then she was gone, leaving the sound of her laughter tinkling in her wake.

Chelsea was still laughing softly to herself as she walked into the room she had always had in the past. Cristina had unpacked for her and everything looked spotless, familiar yet unfamiliar. Like Ricardo. There was something different about him. Or was there? Was it simply that they were equals now, that they related differently to one another? They had met tonight not with Ricardo as mentor and Chelsea as the confused, but as equals. They had met not as man and girl, but as man and woman. When he'd told her tonight she was beautiful, he'd meant it. Oh, how that would have pleased her several years ago! It didn't now, not particularly. She *was* beautiful, many men had told her that. Even a few women had paid her the compliment.

CHAPTER NINE

MERCEDES paid Chelsea the compliment, too. She was astonished, delighted, not only by the physical change in her friend but also by her confidence and poise—attributes she had so clearly lacked when younger.

During the first week of Chelsea's stay, the two of them spent hours and hours talking, catching up with two years of news, having the sort of conversations one simply couldn't put into letters. They did a lot of shopping and they also spent time with Doña Teodora who, though she stayed in her rooms most of the time, was beginning to recover after her attack of bronchitis.

Chelsea was shocked on seeing Teodora again. The old lady was by no means as buxom as she used to be, there was a distinct frailty about her and, though her eyes registered every detail, as ever, they were dull, lacking lustre and life. They also closed often, of their own accord, when Teodora would simply drift off to sleep, be it while sitting up or resting in bed, and time without number this happened even in the middle of a conversation. She refused flatly to have a nurse 'fussing over her', insisting that she was not ill but tired, very tired. Not even Ricardo could change her mind on that.

Except for dinner times, Ricardo was hardly to be seen. He was starting to look tense and he spent most of his time at the bank or in his study. This struck Chelsea as odd until she learned the reason for it, one evening when he asked whether he might have a word with her in private.

'How was your day?' He motioned for her to sit opposite his desk and when Chelsea answered with, 'Fun,' he merely nodded absently.

She frowned at the huge amount of files and papers

on his desk, at his obvious preoccupation. 'This isn't like you, Ricardo. I've never known you bury yourself in work before. You've always made it your business to——'

'I know.' He cut her off, running a hand tiredly through his hair. 'It's this damned lecture tour.'

'Lecture tour?'

'It's been timed to coincide with the publication of my book. I shall be going round the country, and I mean literally all over Spain, lecturing to university students, bank employees and several other kinds of institutions.' Only then did he look at her properly. 'On matters of banking, finance, economics.'

'I gathered that.'

'I wondered whether you'd consider coming with me.'

Startled, her first thought quickly formed into questions. 'Me? But why? What use could I be to you?'

'Plenty.' He was almost abrupt, making Chelsea realise he really was tired. 'You're multi-lingual, you type, write shorthand——'

'But my shorthand's rusty, to say the least!'

'That doesn't matter. Just listen then give me your answer. I need someone to come with me and I can't take my own assistant or secretary, they have enough to do here at the bank. I've got several deals going through at the moment—quite apart from handling this lot and my routine work. I need someone to be near a telephone for me, to handle correspondence. And you have a driving licence, you could share the driving with me. That in itself would be a big help, it would free me for several hours a day so I can work while we're travelling. I've decided to travel by road rather than air. One can waste a lot of time hanging around airports. You'll be paid, of course. Name your fee. We'll be away five weeks in all. I'm going to take the opportunity to call on some important customers and some of our bank branches while I'm doing the rounds.'

'I'll do it!' Chelsea was flattered that he thought she

could cope. She would certainly do her best. And why not go? She was free to do so and it sounded like a challenge. It would also be interesting to see more of Spain. 'And I'll do it for the fun of it. I don't expect to be paid.'

'Of course you'll be paid. By the bank. And, please note, it will hardly be fun. You'll be working hard, damned hard.' He looked at her expectantly, as though he thought she might have changed her mind now.

'Fine. When will we leave?'

'A week after the wedding, on the Sunday. I'll let you have a copy of our itinerary nearer the time.' And with that he picked up a file, dismissing her. 'Forgive me now. I must get on.'

Chelsea left him alone. She paused outside his door, her feelings mixed. She felt decidedly rebuffed by his abrupt dismissal. She felt excited at the prospect of travelling and working with him because she would learn things, it would be good experience for her. And she also felt . . . neglected. Since the night of her arrival they had hardly spoken to each other except briefly during dinner. It was as if he'd forgotten she was a guest in his house.

She shrugged. Maybe she should be flattered instead of feeling neglected, flattered that he wasn't treating her like a guest. Didn't that make her something more special?

During the first few days of her second week, Chelsea didn't quite know what to do with herself. Emilio had arrived and effectively robbed her of Mercedes' company for much of the time. Of course, it was only natural they would want to be alone when they could. The pair of them were so obviously, madly in love, it was almost laughable to Chelsea.

There was only so much time she could spend with Doña Teodora, so she accepted the invitations which came from other members of the Colchero family, most especially those of Antonia, Mercedes' young aunt who enjoyed shopping and luncheons in fine restuarants almost as much as her niece did.

As their big day got nearer, Emilio and Mercedes began to look as tense as Ricardo, though he had stopped going in to the bank so often and was content to work in his study.

Already the house was decked with flowers, shuttered against the blazing heat during the daytime, cool in the evenings, and wedding presents were arriving daily. Chelsea was on her way out one morning, about to collect her own, specially ordered gift, when Ricardo intercepted her. His study door was open and he called to her as she crossed the hall.

'Good morning, Ricardo.' She looked cool and composed in a pale pink dress, its neck and hemline trimmed with white daisies.

'You're looking very pretty today, Chelsea. Where are you off to?' He smiled for what seemed like the first time in days.

She forgave him everything then, his lack of interest and all. 'To collect Mercedes' wedding present. Then I'm having lunch at Antonia's. Mercedes and Emilio aren't going out today. They're entertaining some of his friends here to lunch.'

Ricardo nodded. 'This place is getting to be something of a madhouse. I'll be glad when this wedding's over.'

Chelsea looked at him more closely. So that was it. The tension of the wedding was getting to him, too, it wasn't only that he'd had an extraordinary workload to cope with. 'I know what you mean!'

'You're a good judge, getting away for a few hours. I was going to ask you to have lunch with me—out! Why don't we go out to dinner tonight, just the two of us?'

She wanted very much to say yes, knowing full well that this was not the offer of a date so much as his need for escape. 'I—well, I can't. I have a date tonight.'

The word brought his eyebrows up slightly. Indeed? he asked silently. 'A date?'

'Mm. With Miguel Buendia.' She laughed a little, remembering her first meeting with Miguel, at the party Ricardo had taken her to when she was eighteen. She hadn't looked at him twice on that occasion, thinking him archaic at the time! Now, however, she thought him interesting. 'He was in the restaurant where Antonia and I went to lunch a couple of days ago. He asked us to join him, he remembered meeting me before and——'

'I'll bet he did. You needn't bother to explain.' There was an edge to Ricardo's voice. The smile had faded from his lips and he looked annoyed. 'Didn't Antonia advise you against the idea?'

'No!' Chelsea stared at him in surprise. What on earth was he thinking about? 'Why should she? Is he married or something?'

'Not likely! He enjoys his women too much for that. Why buy a book when you can borrow from an entire library ... that's Miguel's philosophy. His reputation is——'

'I'm not interested, thank you!' He had to be exaggerating, Antonia *would* have said something if Miguel were known to be some kind of wolf where women were concerned.

Ricardo ignored her outburst. 'Well, I'm advising you. And I'm warning you, you'll regret it if you go out with him. You can't handle the type——'

Anger flared up in her. 'What would you know about what I can handle? I'm not seventeen years old any longer, kindly remember that and don't interfere!'

'I see!' For the first time ever, he raised his voice to her. 'I see you're as stubborn as you always were! Can't you take my word that——'

Before he could finish, Mercedes' voice reached them from the other side of the hall. It was tinged with panic. 'What's the matter with you two?'

Chelsea turned, smiling. She was anxious to placate her friend because she was worrying over the smallest thing these days. 'Nothing, Merc. Just a difference of opinion. Ricardo seems to think it's a bad idea for me to go out with Miguel Buendia tonight, seems to think he's some kind of Bluebeard!'

Mercedes looked curiously at her brother. 'Well, I think that's rather unfair——'

'Your opinion was not invited, Mercedes!' Ricardo snapped harshly. 'What do you know about Miguel? Now go about your business!'

Her eyes widening, Mercedes mumbled an apology and retreated.

Chelsea spun round, furious now. 'What the hell's the matter with you? That girl is a nervous wreck and you yell at her like that! I see *you're* as autocratic as ever! Well, *I* never took orders from you, Ricardo, and I'm damned if I'll start now!'

'Chelsea! Wait——'

She did not wait. To think she had considered cancelling her date, to go out with him! She was really annoyed now. Being told not to do something only made her more determined to assert herself. In that respect, he was right, she hadn't changed. She flounced out of the hall without even looking back.

She saw Mercedes later in the day, but not Ricardo. She was disappointed about that. Some residue of childishness in her wanted to press home the point she'd made to him. She had dressed to the nines for her date with Miguel and she wanted Ricardo to see that.

He did, eventually. It was during the early hours of the morning. He was sitting in the main salon when she got in from her date. It was turned one o'clock and she might never have known he'd waited up—if he hadn't summoned her as she approached the staircase!

'Chelsea? I want a word.'

Instantly seeing red, her annoyance with him came back with a vengeance. She could hardly believe this! She said as much. She marched into the room and shut the door, her temper bringing added colour to her cheeks. 'I don't believe it! Playing nursemaid, are you? Do you think you can monitor me as you monitor your sister? You've waited up to see whether I'm in one piece, is that it?'

'Don't be ridiculous.' Ricardo spoke coolly. He seemed far more relaxed tonight. Much to her chagrin, she soon found out why. 'I've been out myself. I've been home for precisely five minutes and I'm having a nightcap. I merely wondered whether you'd like one.'

'Oh!'

'Oh!' he mocked. 'So what would you like to drink while you make your apology?'

'Nothing. I——' Apology? She wasn't going to apologise for her assumption, even if she was wrong in having made it! She sighed inwardly, realising that was illogical and unfair. It seemed as though wedding nerves were getting to everyone, herself included. Once more there was tension in the air, and she didn't like it. She was on the verge of apologising when it all went wrong again.

Ricardo, now seated, let his eyes roam slowly over her from top to toe. 'You certainly went to town with your choice of dress tonight. Perhaps I have quite the wrong impression of you, Chelsea? Perhaps Miguel Buendia is the type you go for these days? Maybe you like a good time as much as he does? After all, you once said that was all you wanted when you left the finishing school.'

Chelsea couldn't believe her ears. What on earth was he saying, implying? Surely he was needling her deliberately? His eyes were on the swell of her breasts in the low-cut dress she had deliberately chosen. The flush in her cheeks deepened. She felt as if she didn't know him at all. Perhaps she didn't. Their relationship had certainly been—different—since she'd been here.

She lifted her head, wishing she'd worn something else but determined not to explain anything at all. Why should she? He could think what he liked! Miguel

Buendia had behaved like a perfect gentleman tonight—but she was damned if she'd tell Ricardo that! 'Perhaps,' she said mysteriously. 'Perhaps I do like a good time—as you put it. That's for me to know and for you to wonder about. Good night, Ricardo.'

'Chelsea!' The word cut across the room like a scythe. She almost stopped in her tracks, so astonished was she by the unprecedented anger in his voice. *'I have not finished with you yet!'*

That did it! She kept on walking.

She got into bed in a state of confusion, wondering why her relationship with Ricardo seemed to have disintegrated. In the past they had been such good friends. Why was it different now? She had never seen this—this sarcastic side of him before. He had changed over the years, that was for sure. And yet . . . she closed her eyes, thinking back into the past. Mercedes had once warned her Ricardo had a temper. Chelsea hadn't believed it at the time but she'd had more than one glimpse of it today . . . Maybe, maybe he hadn't changed at all? Maybe she hadn't really known him before? In the past he had been so patient with her, but not now!

She turned over and thumped her pillow. 'Well,' she said aloud, 'if you're finally showing your true colours, Ricardo dear, I don't think I even like you any more.'

That was certainly the way he behaved towards Chelsea during the following week, as though *she* had said something to offend *him*. Perhaps it was her having a second date with Miguel that caused it, but that was too bad. Actually, she hadn't really wanted to accept a second date with Miguel, she had discovered him to be rather shallow. Admittedly, she'd done it to spite Ricardo, she was so cross with him and his implications about her morals. Besides, there was no way on earth she would be told what to do—she'd had enough of that to last a lifetime. It went absolutely against her nature.

She and Ricardo were polite to each other now, no more. When they were in the same room together, there was also tension, tension which seemed to be getting insidiously stronger. Chelsea studiously ignored it and nobody else seemed to notice it.

Two days before the wedding, relatives began to arrive from far flung corners of Spain. Every guest room in Ricardo's house was occupied, as they were in the homes of his uncles who lived in Madrid.

On the eve of her wedding, Mercedes was so nervous that Chelsea felt sorry for her. Vincente and his wife Anna, who were the most recently experienced at the traumas of the church wedding ceremony, tried their best to calm her, as did everyone else. The bridegroom-to-be had been banned from the house that day and was staying with one of the uncles, as were his parents. And still there was an overflow; some of Emilio's relatives had had to book into the hotel where the reception would be held.

Mercedes went to bed early but would no doubt stay awake for hours. As for the rest of the household, it was well after midnight before the other adults started drifting to their rooms.

Chelsea popped in on Teodora before going to bed. She was propped up against pillows, reading.

'Teodora, I didn't expect to find you awake!'

'Come in, child, come in. Is Mercedes in bed? I told her to go early. I had a long talk with her before dinner.'

'She went hours ago.' Chelsea reached for Teodora's hand. 'How are you feeling? Are you going to be all right tomorrow?'

Teodora chuckled. 'Do I have a choice? Do you think I would miss one minute of it?'

'No. Not one minute!' Chelsea smiled, squeezing her hand. 'Anyhow, we'll all be there to look after you.' Her hand was squeezed in return.

'I'm fine, Chelsea. Merely tired, that's all. And you are a good girl.' She looked at Chelsea over the top of her spectacles, her eyes narrowing slightly. 'You've turned out well. No longer the noisy little devil you used to be. Now listen, Ricardo's told me you're going with him on his lecture tour. I'm pleased about that . . .'

The lecture tour! So much had been happening recently, Chelsea had almost forgotten it, she certainly hadn't thought about it. Nor was she sure she wanted to go, not any longer.

'See that he eats proper meals,' his grandmother was saying, 'see that he rests when he can. He's looking strained just now and I don't like it. He worries about me, you know.'

Chelsea nodded. It was true, Ricardo did have a lot on his mind. She knew he worried about Teodora, he always had. She really must try to take all this into account, not judge him too harshly.

'Try to convince him he has no need to, Chelsea.'

'I don't think that's possible. He'll telephone every day, we know that. And as long as he hears you're all right——'

'He will. Mercedes, of course, will be on her honeymoon and will have better things to think about. Quite right, too. But she in turn worries, not only about me but about Ricardo.' She paused, her eyes closing briefly. 'Well, all I wanted to say is that I'm glad you're staying around for a while. Things are going to change around here after tomorrow. There are a lot of changes ahead . . .'

Again her eyes closed. Chelsea frowned, disturbed by Teodora's choice of words. What exactly did she mean? She seemed to be referring to something other than Mercedes' departure from the house . . . 'Teodora? Teodora?'

Teodora was asleep. Carefully, Chelsea removed her spectacles and dimmed the light on her way out, some nameless worry settling inside her.

Yet she fell instantly asleep when she climbed into bed. She was awakened about an hour later by the cries of a child. She got out of bed and dashed next door, wanting not only to soothe the child but also to prevent the crying from waking the other two young ones who were sharing the room. It was Paco who was sobbing, one of Mercedes' second cousins, a six year old. Chelsea took him in her arms, smiling to herself as he clung to her, gripping her almost painfully. She talked quickly and quietly to him in Spanish. 'A bad dream? Oh, darling, that's nothing to cry about! It's gone now. No, it won't come back . . .'

In the dim glow of a solitary night-light she cuddled him and reassured him until his eyelids were drooping and she knew she could safely leave him to sleep. Covering him with a sheet, she turned to leave the room, gasping in surprise as she saw the dark outline of Ricardo in the doorway, watching her. 'What—why aren't you in bed?' It was so late, and Ricardo was still dressed in the clothes he'd worn at dinner.

She closed the bedroom door softly, feeling acutely aware of her own state of dress. She had on a flimsy négligé in pale lemon—and nothing else. She hadn't been sleeping in the nightdress which went with it, had pulled on only the négligé in her haste. Keeping away from the spillage of light from her own room, she repeated her question.

Ricardo ignored it. He was looking at her with a puzzling intensity. 'For someone who doesn't like children, you handle them beautifully. You always have.'

'I—never said I don't like children, just that I don't want any of my own.'

'Why not, Chelsea?'

'I—I told you a long time ago why not.' She felt very self-conscious, at the idea of his having been watching her with Paco, at the nothingness of the garment she was wearing, at the way his eyes were roaming over her.

'So you did,' he agreed. 'And your thinking hasn't changed since then?'

'No. I—why should it? Children are a nuisance.'

'Because they wake up in the middle of the night?'

'No, of course not.' She backed away from him a little, affected again by his nearness, confused by this persistent questioning. The sultry air was making her feel a bit dizzy. 'I mean, they're a nuisance to one's career.'

'One's career? I see.'

Her eyes narrowed. It was obvious that he didn't see. What was he really thinking?

'Shall I tell you what I'd like to see, Chelsea?' He stepped closer to her and she moved further back—only to find that she was flat against the wall and, to her dismay, her heart was beating ridiculously fast.

'No . . . yes.'

Ricardo put the palms of his hands against the wall, one on either side of her, effectively trapping her in the aura of his masculinity as he stood with less than two feet separating the length of their bodies. 'I'd like to see you with your own child.'

Her mouth opened wordlessly. What the devil did he mean by that, exactly? That in his view she wasn't as indifferent to the traditional role of a woman as she professed? 'I don't know what you mean, Ricardo. Now if you'll excuse me——'

'No!' He barked at her. 'I won't excuse you.' He took his hands from the wall, his fingers biting into her shoulders. 'You've walked away from me once too often——'

She gasped in surprise, pain. 'Let go of me, you're hurting me!' A small sound of alarm issued from her lips even before he kissed her. His mouth came down on hers hard, drawing from her a moan at the unexpected thrill of the contact, rough though it was. Her eyes closed, her lips parted beneath the pressure of his and then he was kissing her in earnest. As he'd never kissed her before. As she had never been kissed before. Worse, she was responding to him eagerly! Her mind started spinning as her entire body reacted with an excitement which was way beyond her experience.

Shocked by her own intense and immediate reaction, she wrenched her head away, panicking inwardly. She brought her hand up at the same time but she wasn't fast enough. Ricardo caught hold of her wrist, his black eyes glittering with anger. 'Oh, no, madam! You've done that once before, too, and that's too often! Besides,' he smiled without humour, 'there's no need for indignation. I merely wanted an answer to a question. I've had my answer, so you may go now. And you can rest assured this won't happen again.'

Chelsea didn't rest assured of anything. She was at a loss to understand Ricardo Colchero. He was nothing like the man she'd known in the past. As for herself, dear Lord, surely she wasn't still attracted to him? When she'd discovered she didn't even care for him as a person?

Still attracted, regardless? And after all this time? After meeting so many other men? But there had never been one, not one, who had provoked such a sure and swift reaction from her . . .

CHAPTER TEN

BY ten o'clock the next day, the household was in a state of controlled chaos as the excitement and anticipation accelerated. Mercedes had been getting ready for the past two hours. In her bedroom was the woman who had made her wedding gown, a hairdresser who was painstakingly arranging her long mane of hair into an elaborate chignon, two aunts and a cousin who were alternately fussing and flapping, soothing and calming.

The excitable Spanish temperament was being given full rein by all those downstairs, too. Photographs were already being taken, drinks were being poured, cigars were being lit, children were getting restless, cars were pulling up outside and the housekeeper and staff were generally scurrying about.

Chelsea looked heavenward as Paco tugged at the little bow-tie he was wearing, complaining that it was horrid and too tight. She had been ready and working non-stop on one thing or another since eight, and had just gathered all the children together in the hall so she could give them the once-over. She fixed Paco's tie and explained to him when he asked that his mother was helping the bride and was not to be disturbed. Antonia was with Mercedes, too, having come over early to help.

There was a great deal of chatter and fidgeting going on between the children, yet Chelsea became aware of it when Ricardo put in an appearance. Just as if he had called her name, she looked up suddenly to see him at the top of the sweeping staircase. He looked magnificent, was impeccably dressed and was so darkly handsome, her breath caught in her throat.

'Good morning, Chelsea. I see that you at least are coping.' He didn't wait for an answer, he strode across the wide hallway and into his study, closing the door firmly behind him.

She stared at the closed door, her stomach contracted with tension. She was still annoyed over the scene which had taken place in the middle of last night but she couldn't decide with whom she was most annoyed, herself or Ricardo. He had looked at her just now with a totally impassive expression, as if nothing had happened.

She shook herself mentally. That's how she must regard the incident, too. She was trying to, was trying to dismiss it as irrelevant but it was difficult. Her own passionate response to his kiss had appalled her; she hated to think he had some kind of power over her, she didn't want any man to have that, and she did *not* want to spend five weeks travelling with him.

But what could she do? Doña Teodora and Mercedes were delighted by the idea of her going with him, so how could she back out now? Mercedes would start worrying, Teodora would be disappointed and, to be fair, it would be very short notice, telling Ricardo now that she had changed her mind.

The problem was soon forgotten, temporarily at least.

Mercedes' long-awaited, very grand wedding went perfectly, absolutely according to plan. The sun shone, the bride was beautiful, the groom seemed almost to be bursting with pride and all the onlookers were very deeply touched by the church ceremony. Almost every female present cried.

Time and again Chelsea found herself glancing in Ricardo's direction. He had just given away his only sister, which was something that must surely make him feel sad. And what of him? Why had he never married? Because he's never been in love, Mercedes had said. 'And I've given up hope of it ever happening to him,' she'd added dully. 'You, too, come to think of it. Though I suppose there's time for you yet . . .'

Everything about the reception was splendid, too, from the flowing champagne to the last morsel of food, to the orchestra which had been especially hired. Heavens, there had been a lot of money and organisation put into this event!

'Doesn't she look *gorgeous*!' Antonia whispered as the bride and groom led off the dancing much later in the afternoon.

'Absolutely, absolutely!' Chelsea smiled at Ricardo's aunt, who was only five years his senior. She turned to smile at Teodora, whose wise old eyes had been moist throughout the ceremony. 'They're so right for each other, don't you think so, Teodora?'

'Yes,' came the soft reply. 'Oh, dear, I think I'm going to cry again. I'm getting too sentimental in my old age!'

'Age has nothing to do with it.' Antonia blinked furiously. 'Oh, it was such a *beautiful* wedding . . .'

There was a low rumble of laughter from behind them, Ricardo's voice. 'A fine state of affairs! You two can cry alone. Come on, Chelsea, this is our dance, I believe . . .'

Chelsea stiffened inwardly. Of course there was no way she could refuse to dance with him, not here, not today, but she honestly didn't want to.

She wanted to even less when he took her in his arms as they reached the dance floor. It was happening to her again, his nearness was affecting her, making her feel too warm, jumpy.

'Relax,' he ordered. He was holding her close but not, thankfully, too close.

'I'm perfectly relaxed!' It was just that her usual composure was shot to pieces. His eyes were mocking her now, so very dark and intense. Somehow compelled to look at him even though she was trying not to, Chelsea realised she had been wrong in the past when she had come to think of him as handsome. He was beautiful. His bone structure was classic, his chin square, determined, unyielding ... she had never realised how much so before, how it told its own story. Then her eyes were on his mouth and with a vague sense of shock she registered now how very sensuous it was. She had never realised that before, either ...

The annoyance in his voice brought her eyes back to his. 'What the hell's the matter with you, Chelsea? You're looking at me as if you've never seen me before, and you don't like what you see. Take that frown off your face, look happy, for heaven's sake!'

Never one to beat about the bush, she said what she was thinking. 'I don't like what I see. You're a stranger to me these days.'

'I could say the same thing about you. However, I'm willing to accept you as I find you. Can't you do the same? At least for today. During this past week, Mercedes has asked me twice what's wrong between us.'

'She's asked me the same question. All I can tell her is that you've changed—for the worse, I might add.'

'My dear girl, I haven't changed at all. So what is it? Why this animosity?'

Maybe it was a strange conversation to be having while dancing at a wedding but this seemed as good a time as any to try to clear the air. They had to do that. How could she travel with him, work for him in some semblance of harmony if they didn't?

Evidently Ricardo was having the same thought. 'Look, we're committed to travelling for five weeks together, spending about twelve hours a day together.' He sounded positively angry with her now. 'The going will be tough enough without your adding to the tension, so kindly get it off your chest, whatever's bothering you.'

The orchestra chose that moment to soften its music before drifting into the next number. More than one couple turned to glance curiously at Chelsea and her partner. Fortunately, Mercedes was nowhere near them.

With composure in her voice if not in her jangling nerves, Chelsea spoke quietly but crisply. 'It's *you*! You *don't* accept me as I am, that's the trouble! You have trespassed on my rights as an individual and I——'

His short, cynical bark of laughter made her stiffen in his arms. She drew further away from him in order to glare at him. 'You're doing it again! You invited me to speak, so let me speak.'

He did not. 'All this, because I warned you off Miguel Buendia——'

'It's not only that. I found your—your performance last night offensive.'

Ricardo sobered, his eyes looking straight inside her head. 'Don't lie to me, *cara*, that's not your style.'

'I'm not lying! It was offensive and——'

'And you surely haven't forgotten how you responded—before your highly comical display of indignation?'

She stared at him. Highly comical? 'God, if this were not my best friend's wedding day, I'd walk off this dance floor this instant!'

'But it is, so you will not. Now shut up and listen to me for a change.' Suddenly his arms tightened around her and he drew her impossibly close, his voice a warm breeze against her ear. 'You'd better make up your mind what you want. You're disillusioned because I no longer treat you the way I used to, with extreme patience, which, I might add, cost me plenty on numerous occasions. I had assumed I could simply be myself with you these days, but no, you seem to think you're the only one entitled to speak their mind. I have rights, too.' Mockingly, he added, 'As an individual.'

Chelsea heard every word but for the moment she couldn't assimilate them properly. Even the way he was holding her was a put-down. He had her imprisoned in his arms so tightly she could feel every contour of his hard body. He was doing it deliberately. He was effectively telling her not to pretend indifference, and she was having much difficulty trying to do just that. The feel of him was shockingly intimate to her and though her logical mind was fuming, her illogical heart was beating so fast that she was sure he'd be able to feel it. He had her trapped, here in public when she had to look relaxed and normal and preferably happy, when there was no chance of her walking away.

'And remember this,' he was saying. 'When we're on this lecture tour, you'll do as I say. Like it or not.'

'Will you *please* loosen your hold!' she hissed, ignoring his last statement. 'I can hardly breathe!'

'Certainly.' He let go of her altogether as the music faded again. He put a hand under her elbow, gripping so tightly that it hurt, and steered her off the floor. 'There!' he said gaily, adding insult to injury. 'Isn't it nice that we've cleared the air!'

She had no time to retort, they were too close to Antonia and Teodora and a dozen others round their table. Chelsea was red-faced with frustration and annoyance. Not for one moment had he taken her seriously! All her suffering in his arms had been for nothing. She sat, fuming, watching him lead Antonia to the dance floor.

'My dear child, whatever is the matter? Your face is like thunder!' Teodora's all-seeing eyes were concerned. 'You didn't fight with Ricardo, surely?'

Groaning inwardly, Chelsea was almost mute. How could she answer that one? Teodora had posed the question as if it were an impossibility. 'I—we—it was just a little difference of opinion. Your grandson can be—rather stubborn at times.'

There was a smile, a smile full of obvious fondness. For Chelsea. 'Really? Then that makes two of you, doesn't it, my dear? Perhaps you and Ricardo have more in common than you seem to think.' Teodora sat back in her chair, her osture as straight and as proper as

ever in spite of her weariness. Her eyes moved in the
direction of the dance floor and an odd little smile
hovered around her mouth.

The days following the wedding were curious ones.
Mercedes' belongings, most of which had been packed
long since, were being taken by road to Valencia, to her
new home. Chelsea paused in the hall, watching as
boxes, tea-chests and pieces of furniture were loaded
into a van. It was Friday, two days before she and
Ricardo set off on their travels.

The scene made her feel sad. The house was barely
different visibly, just minus a few paintings and
antiques which were Merc's, but it felt different. This
had to be because Chelsea knew she wouldn't be
coming here in the future. In future she would visit
Mercedes in Valencia. She had no doubt there would be
such visits, on birthdays, perhaps, for parties or the
christening of her friend's babies . . .

Babies. She glanced at the closed door to Ricardo's
study. She was still puzzling over his remark about
seeing her with her own child. Frowning, she
wondered whether she was as indifferent as she used
to be to the idea of marriage and domestic matters.
During the past few days she had found herself
automatically doing the things Mercedes would have
done around the house. She had arranged a special
menu for a dinner party Ricardo had given for some
business associates, at which she had acted as hostess.
She had kept an eye on Doña Teodora, who had
developed a nasty cough, had kept any household
problems from her and entertained her as best she
could. She'd been consulted by the cook when there
had been a delivery of meat which was unsatisfactory,
she'd conferred with the housekeeper on the general
running of the house. It had all happened spon-
taneously, as if everyone in the house had taken it for
granted that she would do these things. So she had.

Moreover, she'd enjoyed it all.

The next moment, she was laughing at herself. Yes, she had enjoyed playing mistress of this splendid house, but only for a few days. Marriage was different! No, she couldn't see herself married to someone, tied to one person for the rest of her life. How incredibly boring it must be! There were too many other things she wanted to do.

She glanced at the study door again, loath to interrupt Ricardo when he was so busy. But she had to. She sighed as she crossed the hall. During the past few days her conversations with him had been pleasant enough—but they'd amounted to little more than small-talk, really. That was something else that was sad, it was as if they were both avoiding any subject which might resurrect their mutual annoyance, sticking only to neutral matters. He wasn't interested in her as a person these days, she was just handy to have around for a while, till he settled into a routine without his sister's presence.

'Ricardo? Teodora wants——' She stopped, hovering in the doorway as she saw he was speaking on the telephone. He hung up a moment later.

'What is it, Chelsea? Come in, sit down.'

'Teodora's asking for you.' She sighed, crossing long, shapely legs as she sat opposite his desk. 'I think she's going to fight you over this nurse business.'

'She'll lose,' he said firmly. 'I was talking to the doctor just now. He's coming to see her. I don't like this coughing, I think she's having a relapse.'

Teodora had barely been out of her rooms since the wedding, she was unwell, though she continued to deny it. Ricardo had organised a day nurse to come and look after her while he was away, which Teodora thought was unnecessary. Chelsea was in full agreement with Ricardo on this occasion. 'We'll both rest easier, knowing she's properly looked after. She'll have plenty of visits from the family, and your housekeeper is excellent but it's not the same as having a professional nurse around.'

'Quite. Tell her I'll be up shortly.'

Chelsea nodded, realising this was her cue to go. Hesitating, she wondered not for the first time how she could get things on to a more comfortable footing. She wanted to be rid of this curious barrier between them. It was so difficult to explain, even to herself. He was so . . . distant, obviously uninterested in her. It was so very different from the way things used to be. Above all people, Ricardo used to be the one she could confide in about her worries, her fears, her plans.

What the devil had she done, really, to provoke this attitude from him? He had said he accepted her as she was. Well, what was she, in his eyes? What was it he saw and disliked in the Chelsea of today?

'Was there something else?' His dark head came up from the papers he was perusing on his desk. 'You can tell Teodora——'

'That you'll be up soon, I know.' Her irritation showed in her voice. 'I'll pass the message on, but I'd be grateful if you would not talk to me as if I'm a maid. There are two days to go before I start *working* for you.'

His face reflected his surprise. Then he was frowning. 'Look, you misunderstand me. I'm very grateful you're here just now, Chelsea. I have thanked you for your help.'

Saddened, she got to her feet. She didn't want his thanks for the little things she was doing, she wanted an end to this tension. 'So you have,' she said dully. 'By the way, are you staying home for lunch?'

'No. As a matter of fact, I'm having lunch with Miguel Buendia today.'

'He's back from Germany then?' Chelsea knew he'd been away on business this past week.

Ricardo's black eyes were challenging, cold. 'Hoping to hear from him, are you? How friendly did you two get, exactly?'

No, she wasn't hoping to hear from him. She ignored the question. She ignored his second question, too, and his nerve in asking it. 'I didn't realise you were that friendly with him—enough to socialise.'

'I'm not. This is business. He's a customer of the Banco Colchero. *He* asked me to lunch, which means that he wants something.'

'I see.'

'I'll give him your fond regards, shall I?' He was goading her, there was no doubt about it. He did not like Miguel Buendia, she recalled that he hadn't seemed to like the man years ago, so that had nothing to do with her, personally. 'Yes,' she heard herself saying. 'Tell him I'm free tonight and tomorrow—if he's in the mood for painting the town red.'

She walked gracefully from the room, missing Ricardo's smooth and softly-spoken reply. Outside his door she paused, staring at it yet again. Looking at the closed door to Ricardo's sanctum was something she seemed to be doing often. It was symbolic of the distance between them. She clicked her tongue in frustration. What had happened just now was typical, she'd been all set to try to get through to him and it had gone wrong again. They had both ended up bristling, provoking each other.

Miguel didn't ring.

During dinner that evening, Ricardo's mood was more mellow. It was the first time they had dined alone since the wedding last Saturday. His out-of-town relatives and friends had taken their time about leaving, the last ones departing on Tuesday. On Wednesday, he had given his dinner party and last night they had eaten with Teodora in her rooms.

Teodora was sleeping at the moment, having refused any food.

'How was she this afternoon?' Ricardo asked.

'Subdued. I read to her. She didn't sleep, I suppose that's why she's sleeping now.'

'Did she have lunch?'

'Yes. A hearty lunch by her standards.' Chelsea couldn't help smiling at him. 'You worry too much, you know. All she needs is rest, as the doctor said. I think it was the excitement of the wedding that set her back. It was quite a day.'

They lapsed into silence while they finished their meal.

After having coffee in the salon, Ricardo suggested they take a look at their itinerary. They went into his study where he opened up a map of Spain and showed Chelsea the route they'd be taking. She stood by his side and leant on the desk, trying to concentrate, feeling a momentary shock when his fingers brushed against hers as he marked off various cities in red ink. Her hand pulled away swiftly, as if of its own volition.

There was a heck of a lot of driving ahead of them but she was undaunted. She enjoyed driving.

'Any questions?' Ricardo asked at length.

'Yes, how come you're not lecturing in Madrid?'

'I will be.' He wasn't looking at her, his attention was still on the map. 'Several times. When we get back.' He straightened, looking down at her with what seemed like a challenge in his eyes. 'How about coming out for a drive while it's still light? You have to get the hang of my car, you'll find it different from anything else you've been used to.'

Chelsea thought of the low-slung, wildly expensive sports car and some of her confidence waned. 'Not tonight, I don't feel up to a driving lesson right now.'

Ricardo had clearly not expected that answer. 'You disappoint me,' he said curtly. 'I thought I could at least rely on your being honest.'

Very calmly, determined not to get irritated this time, she asked what he meant.

'I mean you're avoiding me. You've been avoiding me from the moment you got here.'

Chelsea's eyes widened in disbelief. 'What rubbish! You've been locked in your study for a month, working for most of the time. That's hardly my fault!' Her eyes closed briefly. Not again, she told herself firmly, not again. Keep cool, explain why you don't want to go out now. 'Look, I'm feeling a little tired just now and it will be dark soon. Apart from that, I don't want to drive your car for the first time in the middle of Madrid. I thought I'd take over when we get out on the open roads, get the feel of the car then before driving around cities. Okay?'

'Fair enough.' He conceded her common-sense explanation.

She turned to go, thinking it best to extract herself now, on this calm note. 'Now, if you'll excuse me, I'll——'

She felt the weight of his hand on her shoulder, detaining her, turning her round to face him. 'I accept what you say about driving but that doesn't affect the point I made. Tell me, do you find it so difficult to have a conversation with me?'

Tell me. So often his questions were prefaced with that. She was in the past again, remembering his asking that question once before. She answered him now as she'd answered him then. 'Frankly, yes.'

'Then perhaps we can communicate in a more basic manner.' His voice was clipped, his other arm slid tightly around her waist and he drew her to him, claiming her mouth with his own before she could finish her protest.

'Ricardo! You said——'

Again there was anger in his kiss. And, again, there was excitement for her, so strong and swift it shocked her all over again. She struggled against him, alarmed by the overwhelming response of her body. *Why* did she respond so when she resented him at an intellectual level? When he released his hold on her she couldn't decide which was the stronger, her relief or her disappointment. She just stood, breathless, her apple-green eyes unnaturally bright.

She pushed her tumbled hair from her face, unable to look at him any longer, and Ricardo caught hold of her hips, his smile cynical as he drew her close again. He didn't kiss her again, he just held her to him as he leaned against his desk, his legs planted wide apart.

Chelsea felt colour rising rapidly in her face. She kept her eyes in the region of his throat, knowing it was pointless to fight him physically. 'Let go of me, Ricardo. Please!' She put her hands over his and tried in vain to disengage them.

'Why the blush, Chelsea? You're a woman of the world, are you not? You like a good time. And it must be—what?—a couple of weeks since you were made love to. Why don't we go up to my room and I'll remedy that? You can show me what you learned during——'

'Stop it!' Chelsea's voice was barely audible. There were tears in her eyes. 'Please stop it. I can't bear ... I ...' Her humiliation was such that she couldn't go on. Ricardo said nothing but he did not release his hold on her. It was almost obscene to Chelsea, she was well aware of his arousal but her own had died on hearing his words and the nasty inflection with which he'd said them. 'Please, *please* let go of me.' She appealed to him with her eyes as well, not caring that he would see the tears in them.

He let her go, his voice rough as he apologised. 'I'm sorry, Chelsea.'

He was apologising for all of it, for everything, and she almost sagged with relief. She turned away from him, her shoulders drooping as she bowed her head and wiped away her tears. What was the use? She might as well tell him what he wanted to know. 'I didn't make love with Miguel. That's what you want to know, isn't it? Not because you're jealous but because you can't stand the man. But you do have some feeling for me, don't you? Some residue of fondness, surely?'

His reply came very quietly from behind her. He hadn't moved. 'Yes, I have some feeling for you. I have to confess I didn't like the idea of you and Miguel being lovers. It would be risky, he's not discriminating, Chelsea. He uses women and he——'

'Now just a minute . . .' She didn't shout, she didn't get annoyed as she challenged him, turning to face him. 'You know the saying about people in glass houses. You've had umpteen mistresses yourself, Ricardo.'

He didn't deny it, he merely shrugged. 'True. But you're missing the point. I'm telling you you'd be *at risk* with Señor Buendia. He takes his sex wherever he can find it—and if he can't he's not averse to buying it. I've known him since he was a schoolboy and I see him around town. You can believe what I'm telling you. I happen to know he has peculiar predilections which—er—trouble him from time to time.'

Chelsea was stunned. It was difficult to believe they were talking about the same person. She did not ask for further details. 'I—take it you didn't pass on my message to him today.'

'What do you think?'

She sighed. 'I think you should have told me this before.'

'God in heaven!' Ricardo exploded, looking at the ceiling. 'I tried to! More than once. And that's precisely my complaint! I can't get through to you. You're secretive where once you were an open book. Oh, you're still blunt, certainly, but that's not the same thing at all. You cut short our conversation on the night you arrived and you've made it plain to me ever since that you don't want to talk. If you're not walking away in a huff, you're——'

'That's not fair! You're so damned uncivilised, I can't open my mouth without being pounced upon! You inhibit me, you're impossible!'

She returned his stare, the atmosphere between them

vibrant with frustration and anger. 'Oh, what's the use?' she cried. 'I'm going to bed!'

'Wait a minute——'

'No.' But she didn't get away.

Ricardo moved like lightning and it wasn't his hand that restrained her this time, it was his arms. He caught hold of her by the waist and his other arm swooped around her legs as he picked her up bodily and, quite literally, flung her into the leather armchair. Shades of the past. 'I'll sort you out, woman, if it's the last thing I do!'

She was on her feet again in a flash, swearing viciously and crudely in English. Ricardo answered her likewise. 'Cut that out! I will not tolerate that kind of language, from you or——'

'Get stuffed!' She pushed past him furiously, caught her stiletto heel in the fringe of a rug, twisted her ankle and groped wildly for something to hold on to. At the same instant, Ricardo was moving towards her but her entire weight came at him with her body falling awkwardly. The next thing they knew, they were in a heap on the floor.

There was only one thing they could do. They roared with laughter.

'Oh, God!' Chelsea was the first to find words. 'Talk about a dignified exit!'

'I never saw anything so lacking in grace!'

'It was your fault. If you'd——'

'Of course it was.' Ricardo was still laughing. He pinned her shoulders to the floor and leaned over her. 'Everything's my fault!'

'But it *was!*' She was giggling uncontrollably. Her hair was splayed in all directions and her eyes were glinting wickedly. 'I mean——'

'Oh, shut up!'

She had only a second in which to catch her breath. His kiss was very different this time. For one thing it met no resistance. On the contrary, as she was gathered into his arms, she clung to him, partly because she had to. They were still on the floor, half sitting, half lying. But it was mainly because she wanted to; Ricardo was kissing her with an abandon which made her realise how limited her experiences had been—with other men and with him. Her lips parted under gentle coaxing this time, permitting the exploration of a tongue which probed erotically, darting, tasting, thrusting as the kiss deepened.

She had no thought of fighting him this time. She responded with an expertise she didn't know she possessed, her fingers sliding around his neck to the thick black curls of his hair. When his hand moved over her breast their mouths lost contact for a moment as Chelsea stiffened, gasping at the pleasure of his touch. Then his lips were on hers again, blotting out any hope of coherent thought.

'Ricardo!' She pulled away, struggling to get to her feet. 'Ricardo, let go of me—someone's knocking at the door!'

For a second, he seemed not to understand her. She repeated herself, in English because she didn't want their intruder to understand what was being said in such tones.

'One moment.' Ricardo's voice was directed at the door, curt and gruff. He straightened his clothes, Chelsea sat in the armchair and composed herself.

It was the housekeeper. She looked vaguely embarrassed and apologised for the interruption, explaining that Doña Teodora was awake and anxious to talk to him before he retired. Ricardo muttered something in reply. Chelsea was hoping she couldn't be seen. She then heard Ricardo's, *'Sí, Señorita Prescott es aquí ... Muy bien. Buenas noches.'*

When he closed the door, Chelsea hardly knew where to look. 'Why did you say I was here?'

'Because you are,' he smiled. 'There's no need for embarrassment, Chelsea. If I want to make love to you on the floor of my study, I will do so. If my staff don't happen to like the idea, they can do the other thing.'

She stood, shaking her head at him. 'I take it Teodora wants to see me, too.'

'There's no particular hurry,' he said, advancing on her. 'I was enjoying our—communication.'

She sidestepped him. So had she. Inwardly, she was still trembling from its effects and enough was enough. More than enough. 'Ricardo, I—I want you to give me your word that this won't happen again.'

'Certainly not.' His smile turned into laughter. 'If that's the way to get through to you, I intend to exploit it to its fullest!'

To its fullest? What did he mean by that? She thought of the weeks ahead with an alarm which was written all over her features.

At the look on her face, Ricardo's laughter increased. He was standing in front of her now, he put a hand under her chin and looked straight into her eyes. 'What's the matter? Having second thoughts about travelling with me, are you?'

'I—yes.'

'But you will.'

She dropped her eyes. He knew full well she wouldn't let him down at this stage, when it would be impossible to find a replacement. Nor was she going to feel threatened by him. He *had* got power over her—but maybe he didn't realise it. If she used her brains . . . well, there was more than one way of staving off unwanted advances. Very deliberately she removed his hand from her face. 'You know, if I were to make love with you, I would hate myself in the morning.'

'Is that a fact?' He clearly didn't believe her for an instant. He didn't even ask her why.

She told him anyway. 'Physical attraction is no big deal, you know that, so I don't know why you're looking amused. It happens randomly, it's indiscriminate. Personally I've reached the stage where there has to be other dimensions in the relationship for it to be at all satisfactory.' Not for a moment did she falter in her impromptu speech, though where her inspiration came from, she had no idea. She saw Ricardo's eyebrows go up but she could no longer tell whether or not he believed what she was saying.

'That's lacking between us, Ricardo—other dimensions. You see, you are not my type. There's no *intellectual* communication with us, none whatsoever. Oh, sure,' she conceded with throw-away nonchalance, 'the physical pull is there. But so what? I can't speak for you, of course, but I personally don't function at the base level of animals.'

His response was a low whistle; his face remained implacable. 'Well, well. An emasculating lecture, if ever I heard one. If you treated Miguel to something similar, I begin to feel sorry for him. He's already sufficiently insecure about his masculinity that he has to go around proving it all the time . . .' He turned away, clicking his tongue and shaking his head as he reached for his jacket, feigning great concern for the man he disliked. 'Poor old Miguel! That would certainly explain the curious remark he made about you.'

Chelsea's eyes moved swiftly to his back as he shrugged into his jacket. 'What remark?'

'Oh, he asked how you were and . . . now where did I put those chocolates I got for Teodora?'

'And *what*?'

'Mm? Oh, yes—Miguel. He referred to you as my "frosty little Anglo-American houseguest". I begin to understand why.'

Chelsea was speechless. Had she been able to move, she'd have thrown something at Ricardo. What a devious swine he was! So he'd known all along that nothing had happened between her and Miguel! 'You bastard,' she managed when she could find her voice.

He turned, smiling at her. 'Why? Because I happen to know better? There's nothing frosty about you, woman, even if your physical attraction to me does go against your *better* instincts. But I'll tell you what I'll do,' he added, clearly enjoying himself, 'by way of a compromise. I'll let you be the one to take the initiative next time. How does that sound? That should go some way to satisfying your ... rights as an individual, maybe even your intellectual need, eh, *cara*? You may make a pass at me any time you like—the next time we're in the throes of a stimulating conversation, perhaps.'

He would wait for *her* to take the initiative? She didn't know whether to strike him or whether to laugh at him. She lifted her head, her voice like ice as she disabused him. 'Then you'll wait a very long time, Ricardo *dear*.'

CHAPTER ELEVEN

'I'M impressed, Chelsea, not only by your driving but by your efficiency. You have hidden talents. You're doing a damn good job and I'm really grateful to you.'

The remarks were so unexpected, Chelsea almost veered off the road. This, after nearly two hectic weeks during which Ricardo had not once spoken of his appreciation—let alone paid her compliments! Their first stop after leaving Madrid had been Segovia, after that they had driven directly north again to Santander. From there they'd gone down to Valladolid to see a customer, at whose home they had stayed for two nights, then south-west to Salamanca, on to Caceres. Now they were heading south-east from Caceres to Cordoba. It was several hundred miles.

She glanced at Ricardo, smiling her satisfaction, but he had his eyes closed. He was sprawled in the reclining passenger seat and she had in fact thought him asleep before he'd spoken. 'Why thank you, kind sir!' The pleasure in her voice was unmistakable. She had time to see the answering twitch of his lips before turning her attention back to the road.

The Aston Martin Lagonda was a dream to drive. Chelsea handled it easily; all it had needed was a bit of practice to get the hang of it, and she'd had plenty of that by now! She didn't handle it as well as Ricardo did, nor did she drive as fast even on the open roads, but she was more than competent. Oh, and she was so enjoying herself! She was in love with Spain. The past two weeks had been hard and hot but she wouldn't have missed them for the world.

When next she glanced at her passenger, his breathing and the attitude of his body told her he was asleep. They had both worked hard. If he were impressed with her, what was it she felt about him? A new respect. Admiration.

It had been in Salamanca that she had first heard him lecture. The University of Salamanca was founded in 1230 and is the oldest in Spain. There, in that ancient seat of learning, Chelsea had enjoyed with Ricardo the warmest of welcomes and the typical Spanish hospitality with which she was already familiar. And she had enjoyed prestige. This, because she was the 'assistant' to Ricardo Juan Antonio Colchero de Castilla. Incredible though it seemed, she hadn't fully appreciated quite how important the Colchero name was in Spain. Moreover, she hadn't realised the esteem in which Ricardo Colchero was held. He was a financial wizard. He had given several radio interviews which Chelsea had listened to, talking about the economics of the nation and answering questions she hadn't even understood.

Intellectual stimulus? Just thinking about the things she had said two weeks ago in his study made her feel idiotic now. During their travels he had answered a hundred questions for her, giving her details she hadn't known of Spain's history over several centuries. This was another subject he knew thoroughly. He, obviously, loved his country. With every town they passed through and every city there was a story, short or long, only some of which Chelsea had had scant knowledge of.

She eased up on the accelerator and very gently brought the car to a halt, letting the engine run because she didn't want its sudden cessation to wake Ricardo. There was time, today, to pause and look at the scenery, the brilliant blue sky . . . the man by her side.

She had not taken him up on his—compromise. In almost two weeks they hadn't touched one another except by accident. They had dined together nightly and twice they had had the opportunity to swim, once at the home of relatives and once when they had a few hours' spare time in a hotel, but they had remained separate together. For the first time in her life, Chelsea had a faint heart. She had been a little overawed by Ricardo of late. For the moment, she was ... taking stock. There had been times when that physical pull she had so casually dismissed had swamped her. He felt it, too. It had been mentioned by his eyes, avoided by her swift withdrawal of a hand when it accidentally touched his. Stocktaking? She laughed at herself. She was, in plain English, scared.

At this very instant she wanted nothing more than to reach out and touch his face, to let her fingers trail along the hard lines of his jawbone. She wanted to touch his eyelashes, long and black and curly, like his magnificent gypsy hair! She wanted to press her lips to his and have him wake up and take her in his arms. A small smile hovered on her lips at the memory of his, 'You may make a pass at me any time you like ...' She laughed silently as she watched him sleeping, the scenery forgotten. Perhaps she may, but she dared not. Dynamite. She no longer trusted herself; she wanted too much to do precisely what he'd invited her to. At the time it had sounded like a joke to her. One that wasn't funny.

But, now, she realised that to get physically involved with Ricardo could well be her undoing. It would, she knew, be something she could not partake of without running risks—risks she didn't want even to contemplate.

'Chelsea?' Without warning, his eyes opened and she was enmeshed in the black depths of them. Their eyes held until she looked away.

'What is it?' He spoke softly, he didn't move.

'N-nothing.' Idiot! How could she let herself be caught like that, watching him in fascination? She wanted to die when she heard the smile in his voice.

'Nothing? Are you sure about that?'

'Absolutely.' She thrust the gear-lever into place and

took off with a squeal of tyres that made her flinch. It made Ricardo laugh. She just drove, ignoring him and his laughter, her heart hammering crazily against her ribs.

They stayed north of Cordoba that night and it was during dinner that she asked Ricardo why he was actually doing this lecture tour. 'I appreciate that you're combining a lot of business visits, but why bother with these lectures? Is it specifically to increase the sales of your book? I mean, it isn't as if you need the money!'

'Hardly,' he smiled. 'First it's very flattering to be asked to talk, second I feel I should give people the benefit of what I've learned, since they're nice enough to ask.'

His answer pleased her. She lifted her wineglass and glanced around the hotel dining room. One thing was for sure, wherever they'd stayed on their travels, she had been royally looked after! 'Well, here's to the next three weeks. The first two have gone very well, wouldn't you say?'

'Thanks to you. Not only are you adaptable, your languages are a great help, especially your German. It never was a strong subject of mine.' He was referring to the correspondence she had been typing for him. If he wasn't sleeping in the car, or driving, he was dictating and many of his letters were to people in other parts of Europe. He phoned daily to Madrid, to the bank, for reports from his assistant. And either he or Chelsea phoned the house daily to see how Teodora was. Teodora's health was unchanged, she was no better, no worse.

'I've never known you work as hard as you have lately, Ricardo. Has it been like this for the past couple of years?'

'No, no. And this is temporary, you can bet on that.' He lit a cheroot, leant back in his chair, his expression thoughtful. 'I don't need to work myself into the ground, Chelsea. Neither did my father, come to that.

But he did. At fifty-five he had a fatal heart attack and—and I have no intention of doing the same thing.' Again he broke off, looking almost angry now, as though his father had had no right to die when he did.

Chelsea watched him, fascinated by the black eyes and the candlelight reflected in them. He was momentarily lost in his thoughts, his long, lean fingers reaching up to rake through his hair. 'Ramón never neglected his family, of course,' he went on. 'But he didn't take enough time for . . .' he looked directly at her, 'living. Time for living, Chelsea.' He smiled then, a smile which chased away the shadows from his face. It made her want to reach out and touch him.

Their eyes met and held. She nodded, returning his smile. She had once told him she wanted time for living and he had, of course, understood precisely what she meant. She lowered her eyes, casting around for something to say, something which would shatter the intimacy of the moment. It was . . . unnerving her. 'I—I wouldn't mind taking a walk before turning in, actually.'

'I'm glad you said that.' Ricardo stood, offering her his hand. 'The grounds of this place are very pretty and there's a full moon tonight.'

Before taking his hand, she hesitated. A full moon. She shrugged off the remark. He was just saying there'd be plenty of light . . .

There was and there wasn't. Everything was bathed in moonlight. The stars were out—but that's all they had for company. Nobody else was strolling round the hotel grounds. It was October and the nights were getting a little chilly, though the days were still blisteringly hot for several hours at a stretch. Chelsea, her shoulders wrapped in ivory-coloured mohair, felt no chill tonight. She was acutely conscious of Ricardo's touch, of her hand in his as they walked. It was such a small contact, but . . . 'I've always meant to ask you something.'

'Fire away.'

'How did you turn one hundred pounds into several thousands?' At his look of surprise, she giggled, a tinkling sound. 'Your cousin Juan told me ages ago. Did you think I didn't know you did something similar to me when you were younger? At the age of seventeen you told your father there was more than one way of completing your education. You insisted you were taking off, so he gave you about a hundred pounds in *pesetas* and you came back after eighteen months with several thousand pounds' profit! How on earth did you manage it? And what did you learn from your travels?'

Ricardo shrugged it off. 'I started by buying a decrepit car, which I sold at a profit. It just went on from there, I ended up buying and selling currency, in a small way. And that answers your question.' He smiled down at her, motioning towards a bench. 'You might say I confirmed to myself that the business world was going to be the right place for me when I got home.'

Chelsea sat, thinking about that. 'And what if you'd felt it wouldn't be right for you? What then?'

'Then I'd have done my own thing, whatever it was.'

'Regardless of the family business, the tradition?'

'Regardless.'

She nodded. Yes, he would have. He already did his own thing with his property company; that was his baby and had nothing to do with the family business.

'And that's what I'll encourage my own children to do,' he went on, surprising her. 'Whatever they feel is right for them, regardless.'

'Your own children?'

'Why so surprised? I'm not going to remain a bachelor forever.'

'You're not?'

'Well, not if I can help it!' He laughed at the look on her face. 'Unlike you, I have nothing against marriage. And surely I'll find some woman, some day, who'll have me?'

'I doubt it.' She dug him playfully in the ribs. 'Who'd marry a stinker like you?'

'Another stinker?'

'Perhaps! I think——' His arm came around her shoulders, causing her to forget what she'd been going to say. Dear heaven, the merest touch from him was enough to send her pulses racing. What was happening? Why was it that with every passing day she became more and more sexually aware of him?

'You were saying?' His hand slid under her hair, began a gentle massage at the nape of her neck. She got quickly to her feet.

'I—I was about to tell you I'm going to call it a night now. I've had enough walking and——'

'And what?' He stood, catching hold of her hands and looking straight into her eyes. 'Enough of me for one night?'

'No, no, I—I didn't mean that.' Her eyes moved to his mouth and she had to force herself to look away.

'Go on,' he said quietly. 'Kiss me, why don't you? You can't come to any harm out here, in the gardens.'

She turned, started walking. 'You flatter yourself, Ricardo. I have no desire to kiss you, none whatsoever!'

'Liar!' he said softly, catching up with her and slipping his arm around her waist. 'Liar!' He said it again as he took her key from her hand and opened the door to her room. 'Why don't you ask me in for a nightcap? I have a fine old bottle of brandy in my room. I could bring it——'

'Good night, Ricardo.' She gave him her sweetest smile. 'Thank you for a lovely evening.'

Once inside her room, she could breathe again. She leaned against her closed door, the sound of his soft laughter still audible as she heard him walk towards his own room. Her eyes moved to her bed, a double bed. 'Oh, God!' she murmured. 'I want him. I *want* him!'

Two days later they left Cordoba and headed for

Seville. Chelsea drove all the way; it wasn't a long journey. She was looking forward very much to seeing Seville and the day was perfect, the sky a brilliant blue. She glanced at Ricardo, having to restrain herself from remarking on the scenery. He was surrounded by papers, dictating into his tape-recorder.

She glanced at him often, feeling close to him in spite of his physical distance. During the past couple of days she had learned even more about him; he had told her about his childhood, his travels when he was a teenager, about the business-school he had gone to on his return, about his first few weeks in the Banco Colchero, about his father, his mother.

Dragging her mind away from him, she concentrated on her driving. Seville. For two nights. One formal dinner, one business meeting and two lectures. After that there would be a four-day break. Well, there would be a break for Chelsea. They were stopping at Marbella for a while. Ricardo was going to spend some time in the offices of his property company—and Chelsea was going to do some sunbathing! It would be a very welcome——

'Oh, my God!' Suddenly her fingers tightened on the steering wheel and she pulled her right hand down, hard. Her foot stood automatically on the brake at the same time and the car shrieked to a halt. When she saw the twenty-odd foot drop to her right, and how very close she had come to driving over the edge of the road, she started trembling uncontrollably.

Ricardo was already out of the car. Smack in the middle of the road was a mangy-looking goat, looking at the car as if it had no right to be there. Ricardo shooed it on to the hill on the left of the road and it scarpered.

'Hey, take it easy!' He opened the driving door and caught hold of Chelsea's arm. 'It's all right, my lovely, it's all right.'

'I—I'm so sorry! I——'

'It was nobody's fault! Except the goat's, of course!'

She couldn't make a joke of it. They were standing between the car and the edge of the road. Chelsea looked again at the sheer drop, groaned and burst into tears.

'Chelsea!' Ricardo caught her to him and walked her round to the other side of the car. 'It's all right, it's all right.' He stood, holding her while she told him haltingly what might have happened, what might have happened . . .

'But it didn't. Now come on, stop this. We're here, we're safe. It *didn't* happen.' He went on, fishing his handkerchief from his pocket and soothing her, wiping the tears from her eyes. 'All right now?'

She nodded. The tears had stopped but she was very shaken, still trembling. Ricardo put both arms around her and held her close, resting her head against his shoulders. After a few moments of this much needed reassurance, safety, she sighed deeply and finally found her voice again. 'Thank you, Ricardo, I——' As she pulled away she saw the concern in his eyes . . . and a second later they were kissing. Who kissed whom, she didn't know. She didn't care. It just happened.

There, in the middle of nowhere, only minutes after they'd escaped a potentially fatal accident, they were kissing one another hungrily. In broad daylight, under the glare of the sun, oblivious to the occasional passing of other vehicles, they remained locked in each other's arms, unable to get close enough.

'Ricardo . . .'

'Ssh. I know. Come on, we must be on our way.'

'Will you drive? I can't face——'

He caught hold of her arm, without gentleness. 'You will drive. Get in. If you don't, you may lose your nerve.'

'But——'

'No buts, Chelsea. In you get.'

He was right, of course. Ten minutes later everything

was as it had been before she spotted the goat. Almost everything. She had been in his arms again and . . . and nothing was the same. Had she kissed him? Probably. She hadn't exactly been thinking straight.

It was less than an hour later when she had to interrupt Ricardo to ask for directions to their hotel.

He stretched, told her to pull over. 'I'll drive now, it'll be easier than directing you.'

Not sorry to be a passenger again, Chelsea concentrated on the sights. Like Cordoba, Seville was situated on the river Guadalquivir. Here she would see the old Moorish Palace, the Alcazar, and the Gothic Cathedral with its famous Giralda tower, which stands on the site of a Moorish mosque. Much of the original Moorish city remained. Seville was also noted for its school of painting, whose artists included Velásquez and Murillo. She was talking to Ricardo about the former when he drew the car to a halt outside what appeared to be a block of apartments.

'Why are we stopping here?'

He turned to her, his eyes lit with amusement. Speaking in Spanish, he referred to the building with a word she translated as 'digs'.

'But this isn't a hotel.'

'They're apartments, you idiot. Owned by the Bank. It'll make a nice change from hotel rooms, all nice and private and cosy. Come on, let's unload.'

Covering her hesitation, she muttered something and got out of the car. She looked up at the building and saw the name 'Las Luces', The Lights. She had thought this the name of a hotel. But there was no such hotel. This time they were staying not in a hotel, not with relatives but in an apartment. Just the two of them. More private, he'd said. Nice and cosy. Well, unless the apartment had two bedrooms, Ricardo would not be cosy at all—he'd be sleeping on the settee.

The apartment had three bedrooms. They were unpacking in no time, having been assisted with their luggage by a saluting, impeccably-dressed concierge. Cases, briefcases, portable typewriter, dictaphone machine and standard tape-recorder—all were transferred from car to accommodation, as they had been umpteen times before. It was the most tedious part of the work, the packing and unpacking.

Chelsea strolled through the apartment. It was, as any good estate agent might say, beautifully appointed and sumptuously furnished. There was only one bathroom, however. She glanced at her watch and went in search of Ricardo.

'So?' He was in one of the bedrooms, hanging clothes in a built-in wardrobe. 'We have an entire afternoon and evening without commitments, without work. What would you like to do, Chelsea?'

'I'd like to go to bed, actually. I came to ask——'

His bark of laughter cut her off. 'Why, darling, I thought you'd never ask! Just give me a minute while I get this case out of the way——'

'*Ricardo.*' She ground out the word. What the devil was wrong with her? Had she lost her sense of humour? She'd asked for that, hadn't she? Why didn't she choose her words more carefully, why couldn't she laugh, as he was laughing? 'Dammit, you know what I mean. I'd like a siesta. The heat's getting to me. I'm tired and I'm hungry. I'm—well, I came to ask if you'd like a snack for lunch. There's no food in the fridge but there's a supermarket across the road. If I hurry I'll catch them before they close. Will an omelette be okay for you?'

Ricardo looked at her oddly, not answering for several seconds. 'Yes,' he said finally. 'Just a minute——'

She stopped. Her days of walking away from him were over. As he approached her he was watching her in that so familiar way of his, his eyes probing hers. He put a hand on either side of her face, telling her as he did so to relax. Very quietly, he added, 'Now listen. There's no need for this. You're—what is it the English say? On pins. And it isn't necessary.'

A deep flush started creeping up her cheeks. There was no point denying it. He knew her. He knew her very well indeed. He knew exactly what was on her mind. 'I'm—yes, I am. On pins, as they say. It isn't the same. I mean——' She was almost babbling, making things worse.

'You mean you don't like the idea of staying alone with me in an apartment. It isn't the same as being at the house or in a hotel. Well, no, it isn't. There are no chaperones, no staff, no relatives.' He paused, his eyes not leaving hers for a second. Rarely had she seen him quite this serious in all the time she'd known him. 'We can transfer to a hotel right now, if that's what you want. Or you can take my word—for once—that I'll give you no cause for alarm. I'm not out to seduce you, Chelsea. That isn't what this trip is about. And to tell you the truth, I'm sorry I asked you to come with me. You're too much of a distraction. You want me, I know that. You know I want you. But I've told you before, it's up to you to take the initiative. I have to confess, I was only half-serious when I said that, but . . .' His hands moved from her face to the top of her shoulders. 'Right now I want to kiss you, I want that more than I can describe.' Again he paused, looked vaguely troubled now, seeking the right words.

Chelsea stood rigid, hardly daring to breathe. The room, the atmosphere, felt suddenly dangerous. The bed, which was behind him and out of his sight, was visible to her. It seemed to grow in proportions, it was too big for the room. A double bed on the periphery of her vision. Pristine, unruffled. Mocking. If Ricardo kissed her, that was where they would end up . . .

Which is precisely what he said next. His tone was the same but the gentleness in his eyes was replaced by an intensity more compelling than anything she had seen in them before. 'But I won't kiss you,' he continued. 'Because I doubt I could let it go at that, not here, not now. You're beautiful, Chelsea. You're a pain to have around. I want to make love to you. I want to explore every beautiful inch of you.'

She blushed all over again but she was unable to break the hold of his eyes. 'I—you were never one to mince your words, were you? Nor I.' Taking a steadying breath, she answered honesty with honesty. 'We're not going to end up as lovers. You're putting the ball in my court. I'm not playing.'

His acknowledgement was the slightest movement of his head. His hands stayed where they were and very gently he asked, 'May I know the reason why?'

'No,' she said simply. 'I—well, thanks for the warning. And I do take your word. We'll stay here. Now, have you—have you got any change? I need some money for our lunch.'

Once inside the shop, she could hardly think what she was doing. Her eyes were everywhere, looking but not seeing anything. She couldn't remember what she'd come here for. She wanted to cry. It was taking all her self-control not to. Her mind was teeming with confusion. Ricardo had laid it on the line, she couldn't help but respect his frankness. God, how she wanted to—to know what it felt like to have him possess her.

Was she crazy? Why, equally, did she want to run away from him, to get on the first plane to England and put an ocean between them? Why did she feel trapped all of a sudden, as though she were being drawn into something she feared? Something nameless. Inexorably drawn towards something nameless. Did that make sense? It was how she felt. *What* was happening to her?

She sorted herself out to some extent during the afternoon. Sleep eluded her but at least she could apply a little logic to her previously muddled thinking. She had to see the job through. Then she could escape from this—this peculiar influence Ricardo had over her. Once she found herself somewhere to live, she could concentrate on establishing her business, her future, the independent life she wanted.

CHAPTER TWELVE

A FEW days later Ricardo pulled the car to a halt outside a hotel some fifteen minutes' drive from the centre of Marbella. Chelsea looked at him blankly.

'Now what? I thought we were staying in one of your houses?' That's what he'd told her. In the apartment in Seville he'd mentioned that they would be staying at his villa on the coast when they got to Marbella. He'd said that if she didn't like the idea of being alone with him again, she should say so. 'I told you I didn't mind——'

'*I* mind.' Without a glance, he got out of the car and handed the keys to a uniformed doorman. The car was virtually surrounded by people who had come to help with the luggage, to open doors, to usher them into what looked like a very luxurious hotel.

Chelsea frowned. It didn't take much thought for her to realise why Ricardo had changed their accommodation plan; there had been a difficult few minutes for both of them in the apartment yesterday afternoon. The incident had been so avoidable, too, if she'd only realised . . .

Ricardo had been out all day. Believing he wouldn't get back to the apartment until five, she had made several phone calls for him, finished her typing, had a light lunch then an hour's sleep in an armchair. After that she'd taken a long soak in the bath. She hadn't heard Ricardo come into the apartment around three. Engrossed in the application of her make-up, she'd been standing naked in the bathroom when he walked in, without warning.

Nothing had been said for several seconds. They just stared at each other. Chelsea had frozen. Ricardo looked angry.

'Why the hell don't you lock the door if you're going to stand around——'

'I wasn't expecting you till five, that's why! Why the hell didn't you knock?' Her retort was equally as cross but it was also an attempt to cover her embarrassment. Her négligé was in her bedroom and to reach for a bath-towel would mean walking several feet nearer to where he stood, with one hand on the door handle. 'I—do you mind, Ricardo? I'll be out in a moment. If you'll just . . .'

Her voice trailed off. The atmosphere had changed. She heard his, 'I thought you were in bed,' only vaguely. He was no longer glaring at her but was caressing her with his eyes. They had shifted from her face and were moving very slowly down the length of her body.

Still she had been unable to move. She just stood, allowing his inventory of every inch of her. Her reactions were strange; her embarrassment suddenly lessened and part of her revelled in the blatant admiration in Ricardo's eyes. Her head came up proudly and she told herself to let him look; she was proud of her body. Suddenly, things were different again. His eyes reached her feet and started their slow ascent . . . and now it was as if he were actually touching her. She heard her own sharp intake of breath, then the silence, the stillness.

As if in slow-motion Ricardo moved towards her, his expression almost grim as his arms slid around the naked skin of her back. At the reality of his touch, she panicked. 'No!' She wrenched away as he bent to kiss her, her eyes pleading, her fear very obvious to him.

He stood motionless, frowning, making no attempt to touch her again. 'Chelsea, for heaven's sake, what is it? What are you so afraid of?'

She couldn't answer that, wouldn't answer. She knew what his response would be if she told him her fears. He would laugh, he would point out to her that which she knew only too well. No, her fears didn't make much sense, even to herself. Nevertheless, they were real.

Ricardo's eyes flicked to the taut peaks of her breasts, which only confirmed what he already knew. 'You want me, Chelsea, right now, before I've even kissed you, caressed you. Have you any idea what it's going to be like for us when we do make love? Have you? It's——'

'I don't want to hear this.' Her voice was barely more than a whisper. 'We're not going to be lovers—ever. I've told you——'

'Oh, but we are.' Ricardo's voice was grave, his mouth, his eyes, unsmiling. 'It's already too late, Chelsea. It's only a matter of time. You won't be able to deny yourself this forever. It's been there all along, this attraction. Don't you know that? Don't you realise that that has been part of the trouble between us? That that is the reason we were at one another's throats a few weeks ago? It's *there*, Chelsea. It won't be denied. It's there every time we look at one another, every minute we're together. It was there from the moment we met two months ago in the airport, and no matter how many distractions we create, it will remain.'

Shaken to the core, Chelsea put her hands on the basin to steady herself. Dear God, he was right! She recognised the truth when she heard it. It had been there all along; she had wanted him at a physical level since the moment she'd met him again. 'Please get out of here,' she murmured. 'You made me a promise and I'm holding you to it.'

He smiled at the note of warning in her voice. 'I'm going, Chelsea, relax. You're one woman I'm not interested in seducing. Not you, it's different with you. You have to meet me half way. I'll wait.'

She had been unable to answer that. She hadn't understood him, hadn't known what to say.

Now, as she glanced at the hotel Los Monteros, she realised the sense in Ricardo's decision to stay here. He didn't want them to be alone in the privacy of his beach house, not until she was . . . she would never be ready.

Relieved to see he was smiling now, she got out of the car and took his arm. One eyebrow rose sardonically as he led her towards the reception desk. 'We'll both be safer here.' At her lack of response, he laughed. 'Cheer up. You'll like this place.'

Like it? Chelsea's eyes widened in pleasure as they were led by a porter to their rooms. Los Monteros was gorgeous, luxurious down to the last detail. They had a suite of rooms—*each*! They were next door to one another but there were no communicating doors. Chelsea's bedroom overlooked the swimming pool and in the distance there were the Sierra Blanca mountains. It was a beautiful view and she stood for several minutes, simply enjoying it.

From the balcony which led from her sitting room she could see trees, luxurious-looking villas and, beyond them, the sparkling blue of the Mediterranean.

After unpacking, Ricardo showed her around the interior of the hotel. Today was Saturday, he wasn't going into his offices until Monday so they had a day and a half together. There would be four days in all in which Chelsea could relax and do as she pleased. After that there was Malaga, lectures and a business luncheon, then they would move on to Murcia, to Alicante, then further north to Valencia, their final port of call. By the time they reached Valencia, Mercedes and Emilio would be home from their honeymoon. Needless to say, it was at their house she and Ricardo would stay before heading back to Madrid, and she was very much looking forward to seeing her friend's new home.

In the meantime, there was this place! She and Ricardo strolled hand in hand around the magnificent grounds, gardens which were lush with greenery, with trees and a million colourful flowers which gleamed in the sun. Near the small lake, over which there was a pretty, wooden bridge, several pink flamingoes stood perfectly still, some on one leg, some on two. Chelsea laughed her delight. 'Oh, Ricardo, what a beautiful place!' She looked at him mischievously. 'And an unnecessary expense!'

'Let's call it a perk of the job. Beautiful . . . assistants . . . deserve beautiful surroundings.'

She shouldn't have teased him but she couldn't help it. She felt happy. Happy, happy! 'All because you don't want to share a bathroom with me . . .'

'My villa has three bathrooms, you witch.' He smacked her playfully on the bottom. 'Mind you, it doesn't boast grounds like these! Come on, I'm in need of a drink.'

They made their way through a tiled patio into the hotel's Bar Azul, the Blue Bar. 'There's much more to this place than you've seen,' he explained. 'But we can see the rest later, the tennis and squash courts. There's a golf course which belongs to the hotel—of no interest to you—and a riding club, which might be of interest?'

'Certainly not!' Chelsea was going to do nothing but sunbathe, and she told him so.

They ate in the main dining room that night, which was full of atmosphere in a quiet, understated way. The service was faultless, the food superb, and over in one corner a tall, dark gentleman played soft romantic music on a grand piano. Never in her life had Chelsea enjoyed herself so much. She looked at Ricardo and thanked him again for bringing her here, leaving aside all jokes this time.

'I'm glad you like it.' His hand covered hers, bringing instantly that nerve-tingling thrill to her body. She let it be; for once she didn't shy away from the thoughts his touch provoked.

'What now, Chelsea?'

Her eyes flew to his. Had he read her mind?

If he had, he gave no indication. 'How about a walk?'

'And a look around the boutiques?'

'If you insist.'

Ricardo indulged her. Not only did they look around the hotel's boutiques, he bought her several little gifts, a belt, a blouse she admired, a bikini. He frowned when she declined to try the bikini on.

'I can tell by looking that it'll fit,' she explained, laughing at his exaggerated look of disappointment.

She took her gifts to her room, leaving Ricardo seated near an indoor fountain, with someone who had recognised him and started chatting. He was alone when she rejoined him. 'Ricardo—thank you,' she said softly. In her room she had found a crystal vase full of long-stemmed, deep red roses. 'The flowers are beautiful.'

He said nothing. He touched the chestnut-coloured curls of her hair, running his fingers through it and smiling slightly as it fell against her shoulders.

They didn't walk, they drove to Puerto Banus, the port which is frequented by jet-setters, millionaires, where British Royalty has been known to stay. There they sat at an outside bar by the harbour, looking at the yachts, the starlit sky, the passers-by. They hardly talked, were content just to be there, together, just to— to enjoy life.

Back at their hotel, Ricardo took the key from her hand and opened Chelsea's door. It seemed that he had been doing this small thing for her for months, in countless hotels. It seemed, suddenly, as if she had known him for ever, been with him always. As she looked at him, the word good night on her lips, she had an overwhelming urge to throw caution and everything else to the wind, to invite him into her room and into her arms.

The feeling went as quickly as it came, was firmly pushed out of her mind by common sense. 'Good night, Ricardo.'

'Good night, Chelsea.' He stepped aside, nodded curtly and walked away before another word, another look, could be exchanged.

The first thing she saw as she walked into her sitting room were the roses. Their perfume was on the air now. She walked over to them and gently cupped one in her hand, her fingers gentle against the velvet petals. As she raised her head, she caught sight of herself in a mirror. There were tears on her face. Deep inside she was aching. Their good nights, without so much as the lightest kiss, had seemed such an abrupt end to a perfect evening, a perfect day.

Chelsea poured herself a glass of wine from a bottle which had been left with the compliments of the management. She had a second glass, not doubting that she'd regret it in the morning. She'd already had several drinks and now she was mixing them. This was weakness, she knew, but unless she did something to still the carousel of her mind, she would never sleep. She was aching for the man in the next room. It was a feeling, a want, a *need* she had never experienced before. Not like this. Not so desperately. Her imagination was running riot, thinking about him, his kisses, his caresses, what it would be like actually to have him inside her, loving her . . .

Loving her? That didn't enter into it. For him or for her. The acknowledgement of this gave her some relief. Falling in love with Ricardo was the last thing she wanted to happen. And yet . . . and yet there had been odd moments of late when she'd wondered whether it was already happening. She dismissed the idea now, as she had before, telling herself that what she was experiencing was merely a resurrection of the feelings she'd had for him in the past. Feelings she had grown out of, just as she would grow away from this sexual attraction, once she was away from him. She couldn't afford to fall in love, with him or with anyone else. Not in a serious way, not for real.

They swam the following morning. They had lunch at

La Cabane, the hotel's private beach club, then they slept in the sun and swam some more. Chelsea was the first to give up, she climbed out of the pool and left Ricardo with the seven-year-old who'd been playing around in the pool, diving and splashing them. She watched them, the man and the boy, laughing, out-manoeuvring each other. He would make a wonderful father, she thought. It wasn't a new thought to her; she had seen it in the past, when he'd taken charge of his nieces and nephews. Patience, firmness, demonstrativeness, he had all of these things and he used them when he saw fit.

An overwhelming feeling of tenderness stole over her as she watched him. She was almost hypnotised, was seeing him, somehow, in a new light. Again. Would he never cease to surprise her? How deep he was, how very much there was to this man . . .

'Chelsea?' Then he was standing over her, his body casting a shadow across hers. 'Is something wrong?'

'No, I—I was just thinking.'

'Would you like to take a drive? I thought you might be interested to see the properties we're building. We'll be back for dinner.'

'Very much. I am interested.'

Later, several hours later, she regretted that interest, honest though it was. She had asked to see his own house, the one he and the family used as a holiday home, and they got to it before darkness fell, after seeing his commercial properties in the area.

His villa was some sixty miles from the hotel, right on the beach, and it was beautiful. It had been designed to Ricardo's specifications, was furnished very differently from his house in Madrid.

'I see the maid's been in.' Ricardo glanced around the immaculate, modern kitchen. 'Would you like a cup of coffee, Chelsea? With luck there might be some around—instant, probably.'

'I'll do it.'

He left her to it. She emerged a few minutes later with two steaming cups of coffee and a jar of powdered milk. 'No milk, I'm afraid.'

Ricardo took the tray from her and placed it on a glass coffee table in front of the settee. There were two settees in the living room, positioned at right angles. He had opened the sliding glass doors and the sounds of the ocean joined them.

'So who's responsible for the décor, all this ultra-modern furniture and whiteness everywhere?'

'Not me.' He glanced around rather dubiously.

'Hey, don't misunderstand me, I like it. I love it!'

'Antonia's responsible. I gave her a free hand. I think she went a little overboard!'

'Antonia? But it's so different from her own home. I mean, style and colour—everything.'

Ricardo shrugged. 'That was her intention.'

Giggling at him, she put a hand on his face. 'You look so serious! If you don't like it, why don't you have it changed?'

He caught hold of her hand, brought it down to his lips and kissed the inside of her palm. 'I didn't say I don't like it.' One by one, he kissed the tips of her fingers. 'It's all right for——' He stopped abruptly as his eyes met with hers, when he saw what was in them. 'Chelsea——'

Then she was kissing him, passionately, hungrily, unable to hold back because it had been too long, too long. A day was too long, an hour . . .

The desire which was constantly near the surface was now impossible to control. Chelsea's need to touch and be touched was something she could no longer deny herself. Ricardo's hands moved almost roughly over her breasts and she heard a low moan, her name being spoken over and over in between kisses. His mouth was on her cheeks, her throat, her bare shoulders. The thin straps of her dress were pushed aside and then his lips were on her breasts, making her shudder and groan with sheer, sensual pleasure.

'Oh, God, no.' There was no panic in her voice this time. There was only resignation. This had to stop. Now. While she was able to stop it. His hands had taken over from his mouth. His lips were on her throat again, trailing a path of fire wherever they touched.

Her own hands shaking, she covered his and removed them from her body. 'Ricardo . . .' She buried her face against his neck, unable to look at him. 'I'm sorry.'

She heard, felt, the raggedness of his breathing. It seemed as if hours passed before he spoke. When he did, she barely heard him in spite of her nearness. He took hold of her hand, guiding it. 'Chelsea, you can't do this to me.'

There was no embarrassment at his action, only regret. She pulled her hand away, eased herself gently away until she could look directly at him. The raw desire in his eyes made her squirm inwardly. All she could say, again, was, 'I'm sorry. I—just can't.'

Ricardo seemed unable to move. Every feature of his face was taut and beneath the tan of his skin, he had paled. He was just—breathing, looking at nothing in particular. Ashamed, Chelsea straightened her clothes, walked to the windows and closed the sliding doors.

When she turned to face him again, he was looking at her with an expression she had never seen before. She couldn't read it. Hatred? Anger? The very idea that he might be feeling either emotion made her want to die. 'Ricardo, I want——'

'I don't want to hear it,' he told her. His voice was strained, not at all like his own. 'Let's get out of here.'

The drive back to the hotel was awful. Never in her life had she felt so miserable. Not a word was spoken. God, how she wished she hadn't asked to see his villa! She kept her head averted, kept looking out of the window because she couldn't bear to look at him. The silence was screaming in her ears. Of course he was angry, and could she blame him? She had instigated what had happened. She'd encouraged every kiss, every caress, had run her hands deliciously over him, showing her thirst, her need to get closer to him, closer, closer . . .

'I want to make a few calls, take a shower. I'll come for you at nine.' That was all Ricardo said to her as they approached their rooms. He handed Chelsea her key, which he had been given with his own by the concierge, and he didn't so much as glance at her.

Chelsea escaped with great relief. The expression on his face, all the way home in the car, was one she would never forget. Anger, yes, and there was more. Control. Evidence of an internal battle. She wouldn't have blamed him if he'd let rip, told her what he thought of her. She *had* behaved like a tease, the worst kind of tease. But she was very, very relieved that he had maintained his silence. Better that than his anger; she had had a taste of that and it was not a pleasant experience.

How could she clear the air this time? Would she be able to? She had to apologise. She had to. No, it had to be better than that. She had to explain, she owed it to him.

But Ricardo didn't come to her room at nine. He phoned her. 'I'm in the bar,' he said simply. 'I'll see you down here. The Blue Bar.'

He hung up before she had a chance to tell him she didn't want to eat. Nor did she want a drink. She wanted to talk to him.

He stood as she joined him, his eyes flicking over the black, sleeveless dress she was wearing. 'Very elegant, Chelsea.' He spoke with no enthusiasm, summoning the waiter. 'What will you have?'

'I—nothing. I'll have a whisky. Neat.'

He glanced at her in surprise, relaying her order to the waiter. When the man had gone, he said quietly, 'What the hell am I going to do with you, Chelsea?'

She looked away. 'I'm—I want to talk to you, to

explain. Can we go upstairs?'

'You've got to be joking.'

'Somewhere private then, outside? Anywhere!'

'You'll stay put. We've got a problem, a *new* problem.'

Her voice was dull, sad. 'What's that?'

'It's Teodora——'

'Teodora!' Her hand flew to her mouth; everything else was forgotten. 'What's the matter? Is she ill again?'

'Not exactly. She's had a fall.'

'A *fall*. But——'

Ricardo held up a hand. 'I know, I know.' He sighed, running his fingers through his hair. 'It seems she got out of bed in the middle of the night, last night, and took a tumble on the stairs.' Again his hand came up. 'Don't ask. I've already asked. You know how stubborn she is. She wouldn't ring for staff in the middle of the night, not when all she wanted was a cup of tea. Instead she took it upon herself to go down to the kitchen and make her own.'

'But how is she? Did you speak to her yourself?'

'No.' As often as not Teodora was asleep when they phoned, they usually spoke to the housekeeper.

'What did she do, exactly?'

'Nothing. She's just badly shaken. She now has a nurse *round the clock*, as of two hours ago. I've organised it, I've given the staff strict instructions that she has to be watched twenty-four hours a day.'

Chelsea breathed a sigh of relief. 'You're thinking of going home, is that it?'

'I was,' he conceded. 'But I think that was just reaction, I was as mad as hell when I learned all this. But we'll carry on, see how she is tomorrow, over the next few days.' He raised his glass to his lips and swallowed the contents in one go. 'Let's go and eat.'

She left her drink, untouched. He was in no mood for her, her explanations, anything. That much was obvious. 'I'm not hungry,' she told him truthfully. 'If it's all the same to you, I think I'll go back to my room and read for a while.'

He took hold of her wrist. 'It isn't all the same to me.' With relief, she saw him smile. 'Come on, all's forgiven. You'll find your appetite when you catch sight of some food.'

And so they sat for an hour and a half in the restaurant, drinking too much wine, talking about Teodora, talking about everything under the sun, everything except that which most needed to be talked about.

They took the stairs up to their landing and when Chelsea swayed against him, Ricardo looked at her without amusement. 'Drunk, Chelsea?'

'A little. I think so.'

'Then count yourself lucky.' He took hold of her elbow and steered her to her door. Opening it, he guided her inside, leaving the door to close behind them. Up the steps into her sitting room they went, his grip never slackening. 'Sit down.'

She sat obediently, watching, wondering as he picked up the telephone and called room service. He ordered coffee for four.

'Are we expecting company?'

He didn't bother to answer that. 'You're going to drink a lot of coffee and do a lot of talking.' He took off his jacket, flung it over the back of a chair. 'You're going to stay where you are and I'm going to sit here.' He loosened his tie and sat down—well away from her. 'I'm ready to listen. Whenever you're ready.'

She said nothing until after the coffee had been delivered, until she'd had two strong cups. Where to begin? She had no idea. Agitated, she got up and walked to the window of her balcony, keeping her back to him. Not a word had been spoken for more than ten minutes.

At length she turned to look at his profile. 'I—the first thing I did when I left—when I went on my travels, was to put myself on the pill. I was determined to lose my virginity.'

She waited, watching him. His face was impassive. He merely turned so that she was no longer seeing him in profile. 'So?'

'So—nothing. I didn't have anyone in mind, there was no one in particular, not just then . . .' She was beginning to feel idiotic. She released her breath in a rush, embarrassed for some reason. 'To keep it brief, it turned out that I'm one of a very small minority of women who can't take the pill. I tried several different kinds and—and I get all the symptoms of pregnancy, plus blinding headaches.'

Silence.

She moved across the room, sat down again, arms folded. 'I wish you'd say something, Ricardo.'

'I might if I knew where this were leading. I don't see what your problem is. There's more than one way of——'

'No!' Her vehemence brought a frown to his face. 'There isn't. There's nothing else that's—that's fool-proof. I—oh, hell, this is . . . what I'm trying to tell you is that I'm *terrified* of getting pregnant.'

'Ah!'

There was another silence. Ricardo was looking at his coffee cup. At length he said, 'What you're trying to tell me is that you're still a virgin.'

Chelsea was examining the back of her hands, waiting for his laughter. It didn't come. When she was able to glance at him, she tried goading him into it. 'Go on, laugh if you want.' She looked away again.

His response was a long, drawn-out sigh. He came over to her, put his arms around her shoulders. 'Look at me.'

'No.'

'Very well, then listen. I'm glad, and I make no apology. You can accuse me of all the double-standards and chauvinism that you will, I'm *glad*. It pleases me to know I'm going to be the first.'

Her head came up rapidly. Then he laughed. 'Easy, take it easy!' Deliberately, he moved away from her.

Chelsea couldn't take it easy, she couldn't even remain seated. 'I thought that would make you understand why nothing—nothing will come of this physical attraction between us.'

'Physical attraction? Is that all it is? Still?'

'Of course.'

Very quietly, he said, 'You're lying. Oh, you're trying to be honest, but you're lying if only to yourself.' He turned slowly in his chair, looking directly at her. She was leaning against a table, arms folded, her nails digging into her palms. 'You're in love with me, Chelsea.'

'In *love* with you?' Her laughter was brittle, too quick. 'Don't be ridiculous.'

His next statement was even more shocking. 'And I see only one solution to your problem. You'd better marry me.'

She could do no more than stare at him, outraged. 'This is no time for sarcasm, Ricardo!'

'Who's being sarcastic?' he asked coolly. 'If you get pregnant and you're married, it won't matter, will it?'

'I don't think that's very funny. *Any* of it. I'm being honest with you, explaining how it is with me, and you treat my explanation like a joke!' She was more than disappointed with him, she was furious. But that wouldn't solve anything, would it? 'Okay,' she spread her hands. 'It's *my* problem, I appreciate that.'

'Hardly.' He was grinning, actually grinning now! 'I'm still aching from this afternoon's—pantomime. So the problem's not exclusively yours. I have to live with you for the next two or three weeks.'

'That's just where you're wrong. I can get a flight out of Spain tomorrow morning——'

'But you won't. You know I need you. Besides, would that make you stop wanting me?'

'I don't believe this,' she muttered to herself. 'Your

arrogance is total.' As for his mood, she simply couldn't fathom why he was reacting like this. Was he serious or was he not? Surely he couldn't be? He knew very well how she felt about marriage, children. And he thought she was in love with him—or did he? 'Look, if you're not prepared to talk seriously, forget it. I find it very frustrating——'

'So do I.'

'Ricardo, for God's sake!'

'All right,' he said wearily. 'All right, *niña*. Come here, sit down.'

Niña? Chelsea stayed where she was, watching as he rested his head against the back of the chair. He looked tired, strained. What—why had he called her that? It had been such a long time since . . . and what a curious effect it had on her. She knew another sudden rush of tenderness towards him, felt tears spring to her eyes without warning. Silently she said his name over and over. Her stomach was knotted with tension; he was treating all this so lightly but it was important to her. Maybe she was in love with him? Maybe he was right. Many a true word spoken in jest. 'I think you'd better go, Ricardo. This is pointless.'

'I said sit down.'

It was the weariness in his voice that made her respond. She sat.

'Tell me, these men you thought you were in love with, what happened?'

He was serious now, very, there was no mistaking that look in his eyes. For a moment, she couldn't think what he was referring to. Then she remembered what she'd said the night he picked her up at the airport. 'Oh. Well, there was only one, really. Someone on the Kibbutz. His name was David, David Lazarus.'

'All right, tell me about David Lazarus.'

'He was a lovely man. He was from New York. It was one of those times when—you know, when you meet someone and you're almost instantly friends. We

had a lot in common, ideas, likes and dislikes.' Spurred
by Ricardo's interest, she went into detail, talking about
their life in Israel, what they did, how much she and
David had enjoyed one another's company.

'You're not going to tell me he didn't want to make
love to you, are you?' Ricardo asked at length.

'No.' She smiled. 'Whatever else I've done to you,
I've never underestimated your intelligence. So I hope
you'll believe me when I tell you our relationship was
platonic—strictly platonic. That is, early on he tried—
let's just say he took no for an answer. Permanently!'
She couldn't help laughing.

Ricardo wasn't at all amused. 'He sounds . . .' he
shrugged, looking dubious, 'a little too "lovely" to be
true.'

Chelsea's eyebrows rose at the implication. 'You
could be right.' She tried to conjure up an image of
David, mentally searching for some tell-tale sign . . .
'Maybe his initial pass was just a token gesture.'

'And you? How did you cope?'

'It was only after he'd left that I thought I'd fallen a
little in love with him.'

'I didn't mean that, Chelsea.'

'Oh. Oh, I see. I—well, I didn't particularly want him
physically so it didn't keep me awake at night.'

'Has anyone?'

'Yes.'

'Other than me?' He smiled.

'Yes.' She held up a hand, sparing him the necessity
of asking. 'Someone I met in France. That was my first
experience of a strong physical attraction.' But it had
been nothing compared to her feelings for Ricardo.
And she told him so. Since they were being totally
honest, why not?

The conversation went on in earnest for some time.
Chelsea told him anything and everything he wanted to
know. She felt as if she had stripped herself down to her
soul in the end. And she was glad; it had been good to

talk to him like this. She had never felt as close to Ricardo as she did at that moment. Nobody understood her as he did, nobody ever had.

Nevertheless, nothing had been solved. Ricardo didn't need to have that pointed out to him but Chelsea said it just the same. 'So—where do we go from here?'

He looked at her for a long time, his expression grave, almost sad. 'My darling Chelsea, that has to be your decision.' He leaned forward, took both her hands in his. 'You must see that. You must realise, also, that your fear of pregnancy is——'

'It isn't fear of pregnancy,' she interrupted. 'Not pregnancy, as such. It's fear of ending up with an unwanted child.'

'Exactly.' Ricardo smiled without mirth. 'Sorry, I was careless with my choice of words. Fear of getting pregnant, then, fear of ending up with a child.'

'An unwanted child.'

'No, just a child. This time I choose my words with care.'

'What? I—don't understand.'

Ricardo shook his head, sighing. He got to his feet. 'No, I'm afraid you don't. You still don't know yourself very well, do you, Chelsea? In spite of all your efforts to find yourself.'

Something approaching fear crept inside her. It worsened when she saw him pick up his jacket and head for the door. 'Ricardo, wait——' He stopped, turned to look at her. 'I—please tell me what you mean?' She caught up with him, deeply troubled.

With a small smile, he reached out to touch her hair. 'I can't, *niña*. It wouldn't do any good. It's for you to work out. All I can suggest is that you sit down and have a good hard think—about us, about your attitudes, about the reason for them.'

And on that cryptic note, he left.

CHAPTER THIRTEEN

SEVERAL days later Chelsea slipped quietly through the doors into the back of the lecture hall in Murcia. She was white-faced and shaking from head to foot. It was ten-forty on Friday morning, the end of the fourth week of their travels. Ricardo was on the platform, his lecture had just come to an end and he was inviting questions from the large gathering in front of him.

She slipped out again and spoke to the man who had directed her to the lecture room. 'It's—he's answering questions, he'll probably be finished in fifteen minutes or so. There's no point in my interrupting at this stage. Might as well wait till it's over.'

Señor Rodriguez nodded sympathetically. He realised something was terribly wrong. 'Is there anything I can do, Señorita Prescott?'

Chelsea swallowed hard, fighting back tears, fighting for composure. 'Yes. Can you—where can I talk to him in private? Is there an office or——'

'Of course, of course.' The man led her to his own office in the administration section. 'You can wait in here. Nobody will disturb you. I shall bring Señor Colchero to you as soon as he's finished.'

When the door closed behind him, Chelsea bent her head and allowed the tears to flow. She hadn't known what to do. Ricardo had left the hotel at seven-thirty that morning; from her room next door she had heard his telephone ringing just five minutes later. Two minutes after that, the phone in her room rang. 'Put the call through to me,' she'd told the switchboard. 'Señor Colchero has already left the hotel.'

How was she going to tell him? She looked blindly

around the office, trying to think of appropriate words. Suitable words. Gentle ones.

For a time she had been stunned, unable to move, unable to think straight. She had stared numbly at the telephone in her room after putting down the receiver. It had been a long time before she could see what had to be done. Finally she'd made several telephone calls and then jumped into a taxi. Ricardo had to be told personally, face to face. And so she had come here to tell him what had happened, to tell him she had cancelled his luncheon appointment—and the rest of the lecture tour. They wouldn't be going to Mercedes' house in Valencia. Besides, Mercedes and Emilio were already on their way to Madrid.

Poor Mercedes! That this should happen just five days after she'd got back from her honeymoon. How *awful* for her! How awful for all of them . . .

Fishing in her handbag for a tissue, Chelsea fought all over again to stop crying. She had to be calm, she had to be supportive. Ricardo was going to be——

He appeared in the doorway before she finished the thought. 'Señor Rodriguez said—Chelsea, what is it? Why are you crying? Why are you here? What's happened?'

In two strides he crossed the room and half lifted her to her feet, his black eyes scanning her face. 'Darling, you're trembling! What *is* it?'

'It's—it's Teodora.'

Ricardo stared at her, his hands tightening on her arms. 'She's taken ill,' he said. It was a statement, not a question. 'And it's serious . . .'

A helpless, awful, animal-sound pushed passed Chelsea's lips. She in turn put her hands on Ricardo's arms—but she couldn't look at him. She didn't want to see the pain in his eyes . . . and there was no easy way to tell him. 'She's dead, Ricardo. She—died in the early hours of this morning. At home. In her sleep. I—she— she passed away peacefully.'

Ricardo let go of her abruptly. He stepped back as if from a physical blow. He was just—just staring at her. Chelsea sank back into the chair, knowing her legs wouldn't support her now she had nothing to hold on to. 'Ricardo, I—I'm so sorry, so very, very sorry!'

He nodded, once. Apart from that he didn't move a muscle. He was staring at the floor, his mouth fixed in a grim line which curved down at the sides, his heavy black brows pulled so tightly together there was a deep cleft between them. Chelsea watched him fearfully. More than anything in the world she wanted to take him in her arms and hold him tightly, tightly, to comfort him and point out again that his grandmother had at least died peacefully, at home, in her own bed, and at a very grand old age. But she could neither speak nor move. She felt afraid; Ricardo's expression was so grim, so utterly forbidding, she felt paralysed.

The silence in the room was sickening. Chelsea was still swallowing against her tears but they were flowing nevertheless, silently, down her cheeks and on to her blouse. She was crying for Teodora, for Mercedes, Antonia, for all the family. But she was crying mostly for the man she loved.

Her head came up, her lips parted in silent protest. She loved him! It was only then that she realised she loved him. It was at that instant, during that awful silence, that she knew without a doubt that she loved him very deeply indeed. Just as Ricardo had drawn away from her in shock, she, too, felt as if she had been slapped in the face. The realisation stunned her. Though she had considered the possibility before that she was falling in love with him, she had dismissed it, had treated the idea just as a thought, something abstract, a series of words. Now the reality hit her hard, painfully hard. She wasn't merely in love with him, she loved him as she had never loved anyone before. She had never been even remotely close to this kind of emotion before. She closed her eyes and said a silent prayer for strength.

'Come, Chelsea.'

Her eyes flew open at the sudden sound of his voice, the command, the control. 'We must get back to Madrid immediately. When we get to the hotel, you pack and I'll ring the airlines ... Ah, Señor Rodriguez——'

Chelsea scurried after him, bewildered. She watched in silence as he exchanged words with the man who had waited outside the office, listening in disbelief as he explained with utter calmness what had happened, that he was leaving Murcia immediately.

Once inside his car, Chelsea told him she had already checked with the airlines, that they had missed the morning flight to Madrid, that there would not be another till late afternoon.

'Then we'll drive back.' He glanced at her only once on the way to the hotel. 'Teodora is dead. One or two hours will make no difference now.'

Chelsea's fear increased. The tone of his voice, his withdrawal from her was terrifying. She had the feeling she was sitting next to a time-bomb; Ricardo was too calm, too controlled ...

Still, she tried to behave accordingly, she told him of the phone calls she had made, that his secretary in Madrid was cancelling all his commitments right now.

It was a long haul back to Madrid by road, and Ricardo wouldn't let her share the driving, wouldn't let her take the wheel at all. They had only one short conversation before stopping briefly to fill up with petrol. 'Tell me what happened,' Ricardo demanded. 'Tell me everything you know.'

'I—Antonia phoned the hotel. She tried to reach you first. She's at the house. Mercedes has been told and she's flying from Valencia with Emilio. I—it ...' Keeping her eyes on the road ahead, Chelsea struggled to get the rest of it out. 'It seems that Teodora's heart ... simply stopped beating. Oh, Ricardo!' Her control vanished, her need to comfort him was excruciating.

'Please remember that, that she died in her sleep, without pain.'

'How can we know that?'

The coldness in his voice shocked her. She reached out her hand, withdrew it again. She didn't dare touch him. He was so close but so far away. 'Because—because the nurse was there, she was going to give Teodora her medicine and—and Teodora just didn't wake up. The doctor was with Antonia when she phoned the hotel. There'll have to be a—a——'

'Post-mortem.'

'Yes.' Chelsea's voice was a whisper now. 'But the doctor is in no doubt as to what happened.' She turned her face to the window and a moment later she was sobbing her heart out.

Ricardo said nothing. He let her cry. He just kept driving as though some demon were chasing the car.

Time passed. Villages came and went. The sun shone down brilliantly, though the interior of the car was cool thanks to its air-conditioning. The beauty of the day was incongruous, a mockery. From time to time Chelsea sneaked a glance at Ricardo. He was functioning with absolute efficiency. It wasn't natural. She shuddered inwardly, keeping her eyes on the scenery for most of the time. At other times she closed them and thought. And thought.

She had never stopped thinking since the night she had bared her soul to Ricardo, the night he had prodded her into some hard thinking. 'Think about us,' he'd said, 'about your attitudes and the reason for them.'

And so she had. For days she had analysed and sifted, knowing it would be pointless to ask his help, to ask what he thought. He had told her she had to work it out for herself, the reason why she didn't know herself in spite of her efforts over the years to do just that.

Well, she had reached some conclusions. It hadn't

been difficult to recognise why she had such an obsession, fear, about getting pregnant. An unwanted child herself, she wouldn't inflict that on anyone. Even though she had made friends with her mother, even though she knew she was loved as much as she could be by her, there was still a residue of . . . hurt. And, she had admitted to herself, she wasn't mature enough to shake off that feeling. Maybe she never would be.

Added to that, on a practical rather than emotional level, there was her attitude towards marriage, her ambition of running her own business, of securing an independent life. To Chelsea marriage was a trap, it represented a life of sameness and, most importantly, a curtailment of freedom. Freedom was the one thing she had to have above all else.

The one thing Ricardo had not said to her that night was the obvious thing: did she think she could spend the rest of her life untouched?

How could she live a normal life, given her obsession?

That was something she had wondered about since she'd learned she couldn't take the pill. But she had never worried about it—until now. No, of course she couldn't go through life untouched. She was a normal, sensual woman. Ricardo had taught her just how much of a woman she was. But her next conclusion had been unavoidable, clear as crystal: she wasn't woman enough for him. At least, she wouldn't allow herself to be. Even with him, she wouldn't gamble with the risk of getting pregnant, much as she wanted him.

In other words, her relationship with Ricardo had reached an impasse. Stalemate. It could not progress. Nor could she turn back the clock and undo all that had happened between them . . .

She looked at him now, on the way to Madrid, and fresh tears welled in her eyes. This time the tears were for herself. All her thinking of the previous days, all her conclusions, had been thrown into new confusion this morning. She loved him. She *loved* him!

So what the hell was she going to do now?

They were driving through the gates of his home when Ricardo next spoke to her, after hours of silence. As they approached the house, he said, 'We should have come home days ago, when Teodora had that fall. We could have said goodbye to her.'

Chelsea was horrified. She was so emotionally fraught, so vulnerable and tender, she wondered whether he were blaming her. What had happened in *his* mind during this awful day? 'It—we had no way of knowing, Ricardo. One thing has nothing to do with the other. Teodora's fall was—was something ... I mean, she wasn't hurt. You told me she was just shaken. Heavens, I spoke to her on the phone the next day and she sounded fine. Honestly. Well, you know, you talked to her, too.'

He didn't comment on that. He merely repeated what he'd said earlier. 'We could have said goodbye to her.'

It was too much to bear. His sorrow, her own. Her love for him. Her private fears. Fears of the unknown, of the days ahead.

Chelsea dug her nails painfully into her palms; her self-control was nil and she had to pull herself together. She just had to.

CHAPTER FOURTEEN

ON the surface, Chelsea was in control. Inwardly she was a mass of raw emotion, confusion. Several days had passed since Teodora's funeral and during those days, she had hardly seen Ricardo, let alone spoken to him. Neither had anyone else. He had withdrawn totally, spent nearly all the time in his rooms. He had taken his meals there and nobody dared to knock at his door, not even his sister.

'It's—I just can't understand it.' Mercedes shook her head helplessly. She and Chelsea were sitting by the fire in the main salon. All those who had attended the funeral from out of town had left, including Vincente and his wife. Emilio had gone, too. He had had to go back to Valencia because of problems in his own family. His mother was in hospital undergoing surgery.

'Ricardo didn't react like this when our father died. I'm terribly worried, Chelsea, but I simply can't stay here any longer.'

Chelsea didn't need to be told. 'I know. I—just don't see what we can do.' She had heard—the entire household had heard—the way Ricardo had demanded answers from Teodora's doctor. He had spent half an hour in his study with the man, wiping the floor with him, his fury totally unreasonable.

The doctor had emerged looking pale—but smiling. He had told Mercedes and Chelsea that Ricardo had reached a turning point, that it was healthy he had spent his fury on someone. 'He'll be all right now,' he'd said to the dubious women. 'Just give him time. We all know how he adored Teodora. But nobody lives for ever, Ricardo knows that just as surely as the rest of us.'

'Chelsea, I haven't—I *must* go back to Valencia tomorrow. Emilio——'

'I know.' She reached for Merc's hand. The poor girl was apologising for leaving—unnecessarily so. Emilio was her husband, it was with him that she belonged, most especially when he needed her support. 'There's no question, Merc. Don't look so worried. Of course you have to go home. Stop apologising!' She smiled at what she was about to say. 'Even you can't do your duty in two places at once.'

'Duty? I *want* to be with Ricardo!'

'No. You want to be with your husband, and rightly so. You've stayed here because you felt it your duty.' And what good has it done? she asked herself. Ricardo was unreachable. She had known he would take his grandmother's death hard but she had not expected this. So much for the doctor's 'turning point', Ricardo was still wearing that same facial expression—as if he were about to kill someone.

'You'll stay on, won't you, Chelsea? Ricardo does need someone to be here. I'm not deceived by his——'

'I can't.'

'Chelsea! He needs——'

'He doesn't need me, Mercedes. I've asked twice if I might speak to him but . . .' But the message had come back via the housekeeper: not today. Ricardo's refusal to see her had been crushing, devastating. Such a short time ago they had been so close, so very *close*. After the night of their long heart to heart, he had been so—so gentle with her. So attentive. And now . . . 'I'm sorry, Merc, I—I just can't stay.'

'But *why*?' Mercedes demanded. 'God help us, Chelsea, it isn't as if you've got any commitments! You haven't even got a place to *live*! What's your hurry? How can you be so thoughtless, so selfish? I think it's mean of you to go when . . . oh, *no*!'

It was, for Chelsea, the last straw. Mercedes had never spoken to her like this before and her demands, her accusations on top of everything else, were just too much. She had burst into tears and was sobbing uncontrollably. Too much. She no longer knew who she was or what she was. Didn't know how she fitted into this household, whether she belonged here now, whether she was even welcome by its master.

Mercedes had flung her arms around her. She rocked Chelsea back and forth as though she were a child. 'Oh, Chelsea, you idiot! Why didn't you tell me before? Why didn't I see it for myself? It's finally happened. And of all the people in the world, it has to be my brother! I should have known. I should have seen it coming. But the last time I saw you there was so much antipathy between ... What's happened? How does Ricardo feel? Is he in love with you?'

If Mercedes didn't know the answer to that, how could Chelsea be expected to? When she could find her voice, she explained to her friend as best she could—as much as she knew. 'He—I have no idea. Merc, I don't want you to say a word, not a word. You mustn't interfere, promise me!'

'Are you mad? I can't get near him, either. And do you think for one second that I'd interfere in such matters?'

'No. No, I don't. I'm sorry. I—can't tell you what happened, how it happened. It just did. It—crept up on me. We—Ricardo actually told me I was in love with him. But I don't know whether he really meant it, I mean, whether he really believes it. And I didn't know it myself at the time, so of course I laughed at the idea ...'

Mercedes held her at arm's length. 'You're making no sense at all, you realise that?'

'I—yes. Nothing makes sense any more. All I know is that I've got to get away from here, from him. I can't bear the way he's behaving towards me. Forgive me. Please try to understand——'

'Of course I do.'

She did, too. When it came to love, there wasn't much Mercedes didn't understand. She looked sadly at Chelsea. 'Why don't you try talking to him? He's in his study.'

'Is he? I didn't hear him come down.'

'It gets better. I've been informed he's actually going to join us for dinner tonight.'

Hope! There was hope. Was he coming round, had he stopped being angry with the world and everyone in it? 'I'll try it,' she told Mercedes. 'I'll go and do something about my face and then I'll try talking to him.'

She knocked on Ricardo's door ten minutes later. There was no reply. Bracing herself, she knocked again and opened the door. The room was empty. Ricardo had gone out, Cristina informed her a moment later. 'Are you looking for Señor Colchero? He's just gone out. He asked me to tell you he won't be back for dinner.'

Chelsea didn't sleep that night, not at all. She lay for hours, wondering what she would in fact have said to Ricardo if she'd had a chance to talk to him. 'I love you'? 'You were right, I am in love with you.' And then what? 'But it makes no difference, I'm leaving just the same. I'm leaving because I love you too much, because I don't want to love you. Because I'm *afraid*.'

And there were other things to be afraid of now. Everything was different now. She was afraid that Ricardo might not love her.

She was also afraid that he did.

'Will you come home and have lunch with me?' Antonia asked. She and Chelsea had just said goodbye to Mercedes at the airport. 'You have time.'

'I know, but no thanks. I—have to talk to Ricardo.'

The older woman nodded, noting the way Chelsea had averted her eyes. Antonia was curious but she asked no questions. Whatever was happening between Chelsea and Ricardo had to be sorted out. She only hoped her nephew would stop Chelsea leaving Spain. He would be a fool to let her go. If he did, she might never come back. 'Yes, you must talk to him. I'll drop you at the house but I won't come in.'

Ricardo was home. He had gone in to the bank that morning but his car was outside the house now. She turned to Antonia and said goodbye. 'I—don't know when I'll see you again . . .'

Once more Chelsea was looking at the closed door to Ricardo's study. She stood in the hall, trembling, afraid to knock.

'Come in.'

She breathed a sigh of relief, her heart hammering uncontrollably. At least he sounded normal. And he'd been in to his office. Perhaps . . .

Her heart sank when she saw him. She had hoped to find him working, *doing* something. Instead she found him staring into the fire, smoking, his large frame sprawled in an armchair. There wasn't a scrap of paper on his desk. The atmosphere in the room seemed to reflect his mood: tense, still. And he'd had a solitary lunch, had not waited for her; there was a tray on the table by his chair, food which was almost untouched . . . 'Ricardo, I——'

'Oh, it's you, Chelsea.' He turned, surprised. 'Did Mercedes get off all right?'

'Yes. I—may I sit down?'

'Of course.'

They sat in silence for long moments. He clearly had nothing to say to her. He wasn't even looking at her. 'I—came to tell you that I'm leaving, too.'

He looked at her then, directly into her eyes. 'You're what?'

'I'm going to London.' She held her breath, hoping to shock him into a reaction. 'Tonight. At six.' But he said nothing, he just continued to look straight at her. 'I—was fortunate in getting a cancellation on this evening's flight. I picked up a ticket at the airport.'

'I see.'

Chelsea's heart plummeted. Was that all he had to say? Wasn't he even going to ask why she was leaving? Didn't he care at *all*? He had turned his attention back to the fire! Crushed with disappointment, she shot to her feet, her voice hard. 'I have to get on with my own life, Ricardo.'

'I see,' he said again. 'I'll have our driver come over and take you to the airport.'

'You——' Her words died in her throat. She was so close to tears, she couldn't trust herself to speak. He still wasn't looking at her and he clearly couldn't—or didn't want to—see her off himself. Her mind was spinning. Her only thought now was to get out of that room before she broke down and made a complete fool of herself.

But Chelsea didn't break down. Something had hardened inside her, she felt as though a piece of her had died. He didn't give a damn!

Though there was no particular hurry, her flight wasn't till six, she started flinging clothes into her suitcases. What had she expected of him? Had she expected him to speak of love, to beg her to stay?

When she heard a car door slamming, she raced to the window, unable to believe that it could end like this. Ricardo's car was heading for the gates and—and he hadn't even said goodbye to her. 'Well, you wanted to know where you stood with him, there's your answer!'

She got to the airport early and dismissed the driver.

She sat, alone, in the crowded airport. She wasn't thinking any more, she was no longer capable of that. Her mind was numb. Time and again her eyes scanned the crowd, hoping Ricardo would show up. He hadn't even said goodbye . . .

But it was hopeless. Ricardo wasn't going to show. An announcement had been made that her flight would be delayed by an hour, and as six o'clock came and went, there was no sign of him. Chelsea was the first

passenger to go through passport control. When her
flight was eventually called, she was the first on the
plane. She had been lucky to get a seat, a window seat
at that. People were pouring on to the aircraft, blocking
the passage, stuffing coats and bags into the overhead
cupboards.

And then she turned to look out of the window. It
was November and it was already dark. Barajas
Airport. Its name was in lights on the main building,
glimmering through the darkness—and quite suddenly
she felt as if she were drowning. It was as if her entire
life were being relayed at speed before her eyes. No, not
her entire life, just the years since the night she had first
met Ricardo, the night she hàd sat in the window seat
of a plane, next to her father, looking down at this
airport, watching that same sign as it came closer and
closer in the night.

An overwhelming sense of panic propelled her into
action. Fool! What a complete and utter fool she was!

Already she was on her feet, her knees colliding with
those of her fellow passenger, an elderly man who had
just made himself comfortable. 'Excuse me, excuse me, I
have to get off the plane!'

'My dear, there's no need to panic.' The woman in the
aisle seat caught hold of her arm. 'I've flown hundreds of
times and I can assure you it's perfectly safe——'

But Chelsea had gone. Almost everyone was seated.
The engines of the aircraft were thrumming. 'I have to
get *off*!' She grabbed hold of a stewardess who was
checking off the passenger list.

The girl looked at her, incredulous. 'I'm afraid that's
not possible. We're just closing——'

But the steps hadn't been taken away yet. They had
just started to be wheeled from the aircraft and the door
was still open. Chelsea screamed at the men on the
tarmac and the steps were clicked back into place.

The distraught stewardess was shouting down to her.
'What about your luggage? What name is it?'

'Prescott! Send it back on the return flight!'

The taxi driver was the talkative type. Chelsea let him get on with it, grunting now and then. God, why hadn't she seen it before? How could she have doubted for one second that Ricardo loved her? Of course he loved her! He'd been waiting for her to—to *everything*. He had been waiting for her to make the first move in every way. He'd been waiting for her to tell him she loved him; he knew how she felt but he had to hear it from her, first, before he spoke of his own feelings. He'd prompted her, he'd hinted—but he'd covered his own feelings and intentions with flippancy—always giving her an escape, a way out! Never trespassing on her precious *freedom*! That was why he had let her leave, without a protest, without a word. It was up to her. He was waiting for her to realise what it was she wanted, what was *right* for her.

Freedom? Dear God, if she had learned one thing in life, it was that freedom was all in the mind. It was for her. She would never be free of Ricardo no matter where she travelled, no matter what she did. Maybe she never had been.

'Be careful what you want,' he'd once warned her, 'because it's what you'll surely get.' And what had she had since leaving school? Three years of—of nothingness. Her years of hopping from country to country hadn't given her the contentment she had known with Ricardo. Oh, they had been interesting times but they hadn't made her *happy*. It was Ricardo who made her happy, it was Ricardo who made her feel truly, tinglingly alive! A life with him could never mean sameness. A life with him was what she wanted.

A wave of shame washed over her as the taxi sped through the night. Selfish, Mercedes had called her. How right she was! She had been so concerned with *herself*, with her own feelings. Only yesterday she had protested to Mercedes that she couldn't bear Ricardo's behaviour. What sort of person was she? Selfish to the core! Ricardo was in mourning. How could she have expected normal behaviour from him these past few days? He was going through his own very private grief, and she had walked out on him! Only now did she realise how very difficult it must have been for him to let her go. But he'd had to, that was—that was Ricardo. He had never taken advantage of her in any way and he wouldn't exploit her sympathy or try to persuade her into something she had to give to him freely, because she wanted to.

She groaned inwardly, realising what he must be feeling right now. A double loss.

Well, at least she was on her way to him now. She could comfort herself with the fact that she had come to her senses, at last. A life with Ricardo was what she wanted, and she was going after it!

Half an hour ago, she had finally grown up.

CHAPTER FIFTEEN

RICARDO was not at home.

'But—did he say when he'd be back?' It was all Chelsea could do not to shake the maid. Cristina was understandably confused by Chelsea's reappearance and she gushed apologetically.

'Oh, Señorita, I'm sorry, I don't know where he is or what time he'll come home! I—he was here for a while. He came home from the bank and I found him standing in the hall. He asked me whether you had left. I said yes. Then he just stood there, saying nothing at all. A moment later, he walked out.'

'I see.' Chelsea was nibbling at her knuckles; she wanted to scream. This was her fault. Maybe he'd gone out to get drunk, maybe he would seek comfort with another woman ... she shook herself. 'All right, Cristina, thank you. I—I shall wait for him in the main salon.'

At eleven o'clock, Chelsea told the maid she could go to bed. 'There's no point in your staying up any longer. If Señor Colchero wants anything when he comes in, I shall see to it myself.'

Midnight came and went.

Chelsea paced the floor in agitation. She went in to his study. On Ricardo's desk was a copy of the diary he kept at the office. There was nothing booked in it for tonight, no business dinner, no meeting.

At one in the morning, she was half asleep, curled up in her favourite spot on the settee by the fire. The fire was dying and she pulled herself to her feet to attend to it. It was then that she heard the car ...

The front door opened and closed quietly. The house was still, silent. There were no voices. There was only

182

the sound of her own rapid breathing as she flew across the room and opened the door to the hall. 'Ricardo——'

For as long as she lived she would never, ever, forget the look on his face. Disbelief mingled with relief. And then there was joy. His arms were wide open and he was walking towards her, her name on his lips.

Chelsea flung herself into his arms and held on for dear life. Though she had promised herself not to, she started to weep. Ricardo held her tightly, one hand stroking her hair as he said her name over and over. 'It's all right, darling, it's all right. You've come back, you've come *home*, that's all that matters.'

It was as if he knew exactly what had happened to her, and even now it was he who was comforting her, understanding her just as he always had. Chelsea laid her head against his chest and told him very simply, 'I love you.'

His arms tightened around her, she could feel his smile against her hair. Raising her face to his, she kissed him with all the tenderness she was feeling. 'Forgive me, Ricardo. I'm so sorry for walking away today.'

'Don't apologise. It was necessary.' He took her hand, led her into the salon.

She sat, clinging to his hand, realising fully what a very special person he was. 'Yes,' she said softly. 'Perhaps you're right. I—the strangest thing happened to me when I was sitting on the plane——'

'The plane? You got as far as sitting on the plane?'

'Yes.' She couldn't help laughing, but she sobered when she told him of her odd experience, how it had hit her so suddenly and with such force. 'Suddenly everything was crystal clear. I could *see*. Ricardo, I've been such a blind fool!'

He took both her hands in his and kissed her fingers, one by one. 'Tell me,' he smiled, 'what it is you've discovered.'

Tell me. God, how she loved him! 'Myself. At last.

Oh, darling, I've spent so much time chasing my own tail, going round in circles and never stopping to get to know myself. For years I've rebelled even against my own instincts, rejected everything which I now know is right for me. I was influenced by my own misconceptions, my own feelings of—of inadequacy, I suppose. You see, rightly or wrongly I never felt loved by my parents, especially my mother. I felt like that right up until Easter, when I got to know her.' She paused, giving Ricardo a chance to comment.

All he said was, 'Go on, Chelsea.'

'I—well, maybe I couldn't have expected my thinking to change straight away, after that. My thinking patterns had become a habit. Until recently, I'd never stopped to analyse them. My parents and their— peculiar marriage—influenced me more than I realised. At some level, I think I've assumed that no marriages are happy. The same thing applies to my wanting a business of my own. It seemed the obvious thing for me to aim for, because that's what my parents did. I grew up thinking businesses must be better than babies, far more rewarding.' She leaned against him, loving him so much that it hurt. 'It's only now that I realise how I was trying to fit a square peg into a round hole. I'm not cut out for business.'

They were speaking in English, as it happened, and Ricardo was smiling at the idiom. At least, that was one reason for the broad smile on his face. 'What are you "cut out" for then?'

'You,' she said simply.

'Then you will marry me, Chelsea?'

'Just as soon as it can be arranged!' She smiled at him, pulling away so she could look into his eyes. 'I want to show you how much I love you, I want to look after you and be looked after by you, I want to have your children, I want to help you in your work, I want to—to *share* with you. That's something else I've never been good at, never really known how to do. But that's what I want, to share the rest of my life with you. I was going to propose to you, actually. After all,' she added teasingly, 'I am a very modern woman.'

'My darling girl, you are basically as old-fashioned as they make them, which you now know full well.' He kissed her then, he kissed her and told her how very much he loved her.

'When did you know?' she asked. 'I mean, have you always loved me?'

'That's very difficult to answer, my darling.' And heaven knew he'd given enough thought to it. 'I loved you when you were younger but by no means in the way I love you now. I wasn't *in* love with you then, not in the least. I think.' He grinned. 'Or maybe I just couldn't bear to think of myself as a cradle-snatcher or something. And yet, when you were eighteen, that Christmas you were here . . . oh, I don't know. I began to think then that there must be a lecherous side to my nature.'

Chelsea laughed and snuggled closer. 'Oh, yes?'

'Oh, no.' He gave her a gentle pinch on the cheek. 'I kept my hands off you, remember?' Then, his black eyes losing all trace of amusement, he answered her question seriously, as best he could. 'All I really know is that I love you now. Maybe I fell in love with you when I saw you at the airport a few months ago. You certainly took my breath away. Only then did I realise how much I'd been looking forward to your coming here, how much time I'd spent thinking about you these past two or three years. I think I fell in love with you then, on sight. But there again,' he smiled, 'I was all too vulnerable because, in a different way, I loved you anyhow.'

Chelsea nodded, understanding precisely what he meant. 'I had a terrible crush on you when I was in my teens, but when I left here for my last term in Switzerland, I was determined to forget you. Not that I ever could . . .' No, she never had. Hadn't she compared every man she met with Ricardo Colchero?

'And I was determined to let you get on with your life. Even recently I've tried to do that but—but it was very difficult. You see, I've been several steps ahead of you recently. I knew I could make you happy, that we were right for each other. But I had to wait for it to come from you. I had to give you the freedom of choice, I had to——'

'I know, darling.' Chelsea took his face between her hands. 'I've thought it all out. And that's partly why you've been so withdrawn lately, isn't it?'

With a look of remorse, Ricardo took her in his arms. 'Forgive me for that, Chelsea. It was the only way I could cope. With Teodora's death and——'

'And not knowing where you stood with me.'

'When I walked into this house earlier tonight, I thought there was nothing left in life. It was so—empty. I knew you'd gone, I could just feel it. But I still hoped . . . when Cristina confirmed what I knew, I just had to get out.'

But he hadn't gone out to get drunk. Nor had he sought consolation with another woman. 'Where have you been? I've been so worried——'

'Just driving. Aimlessly. Everywhere and nowhere.'

Like her, Chelsea thought. Until now.

They sat quietly for a while, watching the dying fire, content just to be in each other's arms.

New This spring
Harlequin Category Romance Specials!
New Mix

4 Regencies—for more wit, tradition, etiquette... and romance

2 Gothics—for more suspense, drama, adventure... and romance

Regencies

A Hint of Scandal by Alberta Sinclair
She was forced to accept his offer of marriage, but could she live with her decision?

The Primrose Path by Jean Reece
She was determined to ruin his reputation and came close to destroying her own!

Dame Fortune's Fancy by Phyllis Taylor Pianka
She knew her dream of love could not survive the barrier of his family tradition....

The Winter Picnic by Dixie McKeone
All the signs indicated they were a mismatched couple, yet she could not ignore her heart's request....

Gothics

Mirage on the Amazon by Mary Kistler
Her sense of foreboding did not prepare her for what lay in waiting at journey's end....

Island of Mystery by Margaret M. Scariano
It was the perfect summer job, or so she thought—until it became a nightmare of danger and intrigue.

Don't miss any of them!

BPA-CAT87-1

Harlequin Presents

Coming Next Month

Available in May wherever paperback books are sold, or through Harlequin Reader Service:

In the U.S.
901 Fuhrmann Blvd.
P.O. Box 1397
Buffalo, N.Y. 14240-1397

In Canada
P.O. Box 603
Fort Erie, Ontario
L2A 5X3

What the press says about Harlequin romance fiction...

"When it comes to romantic novels...
Harlequin is the indisputable king."
  —*New York Times*

"...always with an upbeat, happy ending."
  —*San Francisco Chronicle*

"Women have come to trust these
stories about contemporary people,
set in exciting foreign places."
  —*Best Sellers,* New York

"The most popular reading matter of
American women today."
  —*Detroit News*

"...a work of art."
  —*Globe & Mail,* Toronto